Alicia found that she was trembling

She knew it was a form of shock she was suffering. Alicia had responded to Todd's kiss with passion, telling him with her lips, but not with words, just how much he had come to mean to her.

And then had come his rejection and scorn. She must never let him know how humiliated she felt.

"Who are you now, Mr. Alexander? Passionate lover—or refrigerated boss? Don't tell me," she spoke from the door. "I can guess. And I can tell you this—it'll be a long time before I act the friendly neighbor and seek out your company again!"

"Friendly neighbor," he drawled, indifferent to her anger. "Is *that* what you were being when you came so willingly into my arms?"

LILIAN PEAKE

a secret affair

Harlequin Books

TORONTO • LONDON • LOS ANGELES • AMSTERDAM
SYDNEY • HAMBURG • PARIS • STOCKHOLM • ATHENS • TOKYO

Harlequin Presents edition published January 1981
ISBN 0-373-10407-3

Original hardcover edition published in 1980
by Mills & Boon Limited

CHAPTER ONE

IT WAS A DAY when Alicia had been slow with her work. It was also a day when the particular director for whom she had worked at Alexander Autoparts and Components had been in top letter-writing form. Except that he hadn't written them, Alicia thought, rubbing her eyes. He had, on this occasion, dictated them into a machine.

The two circumstances having coincided meant that she was still there, in the general office, after all the others had gone.

It was not that she was willingly doing overtime—she wouldn't get paid for it anyway—it was merely that Mr. Seager had said, in his kindly, rather absentminded way, "Have them ready for me to sign in the morning, Miss Granger. I'd be much obliged. I'll be no sooner in the office tomorrow than I'll be off again to a meeting."

Her fingers slowed to a halt. Her chin rested on her hand and she closed her eyes. If anyone had looked closely enough, they would have seen, beneath the long eyelashes, buds of moisture that, as the seconds ticked away, threatened to become bubble-sized.

It was the fault of the letter that had arrived that morning. All day she had been trying to pretend it had not come. It wasn't true, she had kept telling herself, that her boyfriend, Jasper, had written from the university where he had been accepted as a mature student.

I've found another girl friend. She's great, just great. Anything goes with her. Her name's Loreen, and we've become firm, very firm, friends. She's different from you, Alicia, in every way. She's a redhead whereas you're a blonde. She just lives for the minute and there's you, always taking life so seriously. She's thin as a blade of grass, whereas you're—well, you know all about your stunning figure, don't you? She talks my language, in more ways than one. She's full of life. She enjoys dancing, going out. Other things, too. Get my meaning?

This phrase had been heavily underlined.

As you can see, she's the complete opposite of you. Sorry about it, but—no hard feelings? None on mine, anyway.

                                                        Jasper

"Something wrong?" Todd Alexander, head of the company, stood in the doorway.

Hastily, using her forefinger, Alicia wiped away the dampness from around her eyes. Since he was some distance away, at the entrance to the large office, it was unlikely, Alicia estimated, that he would have seen the tears. Her hair swirled as she shook her head.

"Just catching up." She did not add, "On my slowness earlier on." Summoning a smile, she told him, "Mr. Seager dictated a lot of letters this morning. He wants them ready for signing first thing tomorrow." The man did not move. "He's going out," she finished, hoping, by placing her fingers on the typewriter keys, to speed her boss's withdrawal from the room.

"How many letters?"

Puzzled by his probing, Alicia frowned. "Twelve," she answered.

"Aren't you capable of typing twelve letters in an afternoon?"

Was the man *trying* to provoke her? "Normally, yes, but—" She sighed, gave one sharp shake of her head and continued with her work. From the machine, Mr. Seager's voice came, compressed, slightly high-pitched, familiarly hesitant, into the oddly stifling atmosphere. Had the air conditioning been turned off because most of the staff had gone? Or was it Todd Alexander's presence constricting her breathing?

Like most of the other typists, Alicia found the man attractive. He carried his head high on shoulders that were powerful. His physique was tough and solid, his back broad enough to bear the weight of responsibility that came his way as a result of being the man in whose hands lay the company's route in to the future.

As she began to type, his voice stopped her. "Are you being paid for this?"

The wretchedness created by Jasper's bombshell of a letter surfaced again and overrode her feigned liveliness. "I can hardly claim overtime for having to make up for my own dilatoriness, can I?" she snapped. At once she was aware of her impertinence in addressing her employer so irritably. She gave him a fleeting, diffident glance. "I'm sorry."

It was as if he had not heard her apology. "Will it take you much longer catching up with your own tail?" His smile was faint but perceptible.

Her head came up and she frowned. Then realization dawned and, in spite of herself, she laughed. "About—"

she consulted the clock high on the wall ''—fifteen minutes, if I go flat out.''

"Then go flat out. We're the last and the caretaker wants to go on his rounds.''

His tone had altered from the faintly friendly to the firmly businesslike. Alicia nodded, applying herself yet again, determined to be finished by the allotted time.

The letters were completed but she had forgotten the tidying up. Ten minutes over her estimated time, quietly, almost surreptitiously, she opened the door of the general office. She did not know why but the urge to get out of the building before Todd Alexander came hustling her again was strong.

Her eyes slewed of their own accord along the corridor to find the door of his room. He stood, one hand in pocket, watching her.

"I'm sorry to have kept you waiting.'' Her voice echoed back at her from the building's slightly eerie emptiness. Did she have to sound so ridiculously bright, as if she had committed a crime in staying late? As if she wanted to divert him from her inefficiency by an out-of-character effervescence?

He nodded sharply. Almost, she interpreted—her senses unaccountably heightened by the shadowed atmosphere of the too quiet building—as if he were motioning wordlessly, with his head, that she should get out.

"Good night, Mr. Alexander,'' she said brightly, like a too perfect secretary straight out of a flashy television production. There was no answer but her own jaunty footsteps, echoing to the elevator.

Four floors down, the caretaker lingered, nodding a friendly goodnight. A dozen steps took her across the entrance lobby to the street, where a wet evening waited. It was springtime by calendar counting, but the chill of winter still lingered.

Never mind, Alicia thought, turning up her coat collar and following the crowds who walked, heads down, bodies resentful of the effrontery of the pouring rain soaking them through, *the dampness and the cold goes with the way I feel*.

Home was the place everyone wanted in weather such as this, but home at that moment meant to her, a letter of rejection, an evening of hating—herself, Jasper, life—long and lonely hours of self-analysis and wondering how she could change her personality into—what was it—one of being full of life, enjoying dancing, going out. . . .

Bumping into another commuter hastening home, a word of apology sprang spontaneously. The man hurried on, tutting, like everyone else hating the pounding rain. It was flattening her hair, trickling down her neck and soaking through the shoulders of her thin coat but she didn't care. Her feet dragged. Why should she care any more? Jasper had gone out of her life. He hadn't loved her as she believed he had. He'd wanted her to undergo a personality change. Lively, he'd said of his new girl friend, bubbling over, "Different from you in every way." The words were going around and around in her head.

Deliberately she had walked past her usual subway station. Her feet had taken her on, and on. Her brain must have told them, "Let her walk it out of her system. Tell herself Jasper's a miserable devil and she hates him. . . ." But she didn't.

Tears were mixing with the rain, blinding her. She couldn't see, so she had to stop and regain her composure, wipe away the wetness. The hotel menu fixed behind a glass-covered insert in the wall caught her eye. Rain, like teardrops, ran down its shiny surface. A handkerchief from her pocket was wet with the relentless rain, but it sufficed to clear her eyes enough to read the items.

Maybe that was what she wanted. "Enjoys going out," Jasper had said about his new girl friend. How many times had she refused Jasper's "Oh, come on, let's have an evening enjoying the bright lights. We've watched television every night since—"

I'll take myself out, she thought. *I'll buy myself a meal, a good meal at a good hotel.* What was on that menu, anyway? *Seafood remoulade, vol-au-vent of sweetbreads, duck farci rouennaise.* She read the prices before she read the translations. Turning away, shoulders sagging, handbag swinging from her wrist, she walked blindly into yet another commuter.

"Not hungry, after all?"

The man's hands fastened lightly on her arms, steadying her as she stepped back, an apology on her lips. Who did he think she was, talking to her so familiarly?

He did know her. With a nervous gesture, her wet hand hit her chin. Once again the false brightness flashed in her eyes like the street's neon lights.

"No, no," her voice was high with brittle laughter, "not hungry at all. I—" She clutched her handbag between tense fingers, as if to keep the money inside. His eyes followed the action. Was he psychologist enough to interpret the unconscious gesture?

"Or can't you afford to be hungry at such a place as this?"

He had interpreted correctly. Which meant—what? That,

although a self-made businessman, he had the brain of a detective? So what crime had she committed this time?

The corners of her mouth curved upward, obedient to her inner command. "Full of life," Jasper had written. "Even if I could afford it, it's an exclusive place." Now the smile was rueful. She must remember to congratulate her features on doing a magnificently deceptive job. Her hand went to her head. *I'm just a little mad*, she thought. *It's the rain—it must have soaked through my hair to my brain.* "Looking like this," she went on, holding the smile in place, "I don't think they'd let me in!"

Her arm was seized by strong fingers. "Come inside, out of the rain."

She was propelled into an illuminated foyer. The rain, dripping from her pathetic form, made coin-sized patches on the soft blue carpet. "I can't, Mr. Alexander," she protested, holding back.

"You're not the only one, Miss Granger." Looking around, she saw that he had spoken the truth. Others were collapsing umbrellas and looking around vaguely, wondering where to put them. Men were peeling off raincoats, women slipping out of rain capes. Attendants were accepting them and carrying the soaking objects to the appropriate cloakrooms.

Now even her coat was being eased from her shoulders by a member of staff. In a moment he would be taking it away as if she was intending to patronise the place.

She swung, panicking, to the man who had escorted her in. "I'm not staying, Mr. Alexander. Please explain to the doorman. I was on my way home, really, except that—"

"Except that you were walking *away* from your subway station."

Alicia stared. "How do you know my route home?" As she spoke, her coat was whisked away.

He answered with a command. "Come up to my room. You can borrow a towel and dry your hair."

"Look, Mr. Alexander," she answered, pulling back from the fingers of steel that had found her arm again, "I'm not staying. I told you. I couldn't afford this hotel's prices. I only stopped to—to—"

"Wipe away the tears?"

The man's powers of observation left her gasping. All the same she retorted, "No, the rain. I never intended—"

They were in the elevator before she knew she had walked the few paces to it.

He pressed the button for the third floor. Even her skirt was wet at the hem, while her pale pink shirt-blouse touched wetly on her shoulders. The shiver came before she could control it. Was it only the dampness that had produced the shudder, or the ice-cold eyes of the man who had forcibly brought her there?

To break the unnerving silence, during which his impersonal gaze never left her face, she asked, "Why do you have a room here, Mr. Alexander?" Her voice had gone small again, assuming its natural, serious tone. "Is it," she asked, switching quickly and producing her brittle smile, "for use when you have an evening on the town?"

The elevator doors opened and they stepped into a carpeted corridor. His hand touching her wrist gestured "This way". As they walked, he stated emotionlessly, "Four months ago I came south from the north of England, bringing the firm's head office with me to Central London. I hadn't decided where I wanted to live. Hotel accommodation seemed the best solution until I'd made my decision."

He used the key and the door opened. His arm swung politely, inviting her in. In the bright new role she had assumed—how long she could keep up the pose she did not know—she decided a really positive response was called for to the cajoling comforts of the room.

"Oh," her palms touched, "how beautiful, Mr. Alexander. How—how elegant." Turning to him, her eyes shone. "I can't think of a better word. It's luxury. All this—" indicating the large bed, the built-in dressing table, the illuminated ceiling, the large specially-furnished area that could be used by a businessman for written work. "It's breathtaking! Oh, and—" she peered into the blue-tiled bathroom "—this, all to yourself."

Her hands were clasped under her chin and she swung a dazzling smile to her host. In his eyes was a narrow look. The full lips twitched then his face assumed its customary impassivity. "Oh," she went on, her false cheerfulness persisting, "there's double-glazing in the bedroom to keep out the traffic noise. And there's a color television. And there are lights *everywhere*!"

"Haven't you ever been in a hotel bedroom before?" The dry question came from a cynically curved mouth.

"Oh, yes," Alicia gushed. "But—" Her arms lifted, indicating an awe-filled admiration of the luxury around her. She shook her head as if words failed her.

"Don't you think, Miss Granger, you'd better dry your hair?"

It was spoken with a touch of amused indulgence, but held a faintly veiled hint that that, after all, was why she was there.

To her own annoyance she colored deeply, since this undermined her intrepid efforts to appear laughter-loving and "full of life." How she was coming to hate Jasper's words! "Yes, of course," she said, "I'm sorry. Which towel? Does it matter?"

Her voice had gone flat, like her hair under the impact of the rain. She stood in the bathroom door, hovering uncertainly. Her false self had deserted her and she shivered as remembrance of the letter, the heavy hanging day that followed its receipt, plus the sudden soaking, caught up with her.

"Any will do," he answered. "They change the towels each morning. Twice a day if I wanted." He eyed the long, fair, wet strands. "Would a hair dryer help?"

"It would, but—"

One hand in his pocket, he called reception. "A hair dryer is required in room three-two-one. Thanks." Turning from the telephone, he said, "While you're waiting, give yourself a rub. There's nothing I can do about your clothes. Unless—" He glanced at his silk robe hanging on the door.

Wear his clothes? Alicia's cheeks burned. "No, thank you," she said stiltedly and hid her face in the folds of the thick, rough towel. Rubbing madly, using both hands, she had to come up for air.

Still holding the towel, she looked in the bathroom mirror and laughed. It was, for the first time that evening, a genuine laugh and it put a light in her deep blue eyes like a match to candle. "My hair's like a bush."

Still smiling, the laughter warm in her throat, she looked at her host like a child putting on her mother's lipstick and saying, "Look at me."

Something about her reached him and his eyes lighted

up like spontaneous combustion between two highly inflammable chemicals. Somewhere—was it in her ears, her imagination, or in her heart—an explosion occurred. Her mischievous grin brought about a curving of his mouth until it grew into an uninhibited smile. The ice in which his personality seemed continually to be encased must surely be melting, Alicia thought. Just for a moment, a swift, passing moment, boss and employee had turned into man and woman.

There was a discreet knock at the door. The tension in the atmosphere, which had come from nowhere, evaporated. He walked across to open the door and Alicia hid behind the shower curtain. There was a murmur of thanks and the door closed.

"Why are you hiding as if you were a stowaway on a cruise liner?"

Alicia freed herself from the clinging plastic curtain and emerged, her color still high. "I was trying not to embarrass you by letting myself be seen."

"You think a man's reputation is damaged by having a woman in his room?" The question was asked dryly.

She picked up the hair dryer and looked vaguely around for a socket in the wall of the bedroom. "I don't know. I've never been in a man's room before. Not in these circumstances." She spoke abstractedly, remembering that she needed a comb.

For a moment she gave her mind to the consideration of his question. "No, that was a bit naive. At twenty-three that's something I'm certainly not. On thinking about it," she smiled up at him, "I guess it actually *enhances* his reputation. Reveals his virility, tells the world that he's a very male animal."

Having found a wall socket, she pushed in the plug.

Both hands were thrust into pockets as he commented, giving her a strangely assessing look, "You seem to have it all worked out. I assume you have personal experience of these matters?" An eyebrow was lifted in cynical inquiry.

"No, Mr. Alexander, none at all."

He came closer, brown eyes looking her over. To dry her blouse more quickly, she had unfastened two or three buttons, thus creating a plunging neckline. Her instinct was to refasten them, but in her assumed role of animated, life-loving womanhood, she held back her twitching fingers. If he saw more than Jasper had ever been allowed to see, then wouldn't she be acting like most other girls of her age, which Jasper's letter had implied she was too prudish to do. His new girl, Loreen, however, was "just great." *Anything* went with her, he'd said. So the buttons stayed undone and Todd Alexander looked his fill at the rounded shapes plainly outlined beneath the shirt-blouse.

Looking for the switch on the hand-held hair dryer, she heard him say, "A girl with all your physical assets couldn't have reached twenty-three without gathering some closer-than-brotherly knowledge of men. You must, at some time, have acquired yourself a boyfriend."

With her finger on the switch, she smiled up at him, part herself, part animated actress. "Since they were statements, not questions, Mr. Alexander, they don't require an answer, do they?" When she switched on the hair dryer, she switched off her smile. Her bag lay on the bed, and she took a comb from it, running the raking teeth through her damp hair. The warm stream of air blew the blond cloud into controlled curls and attractive fullness.

Her host moved away, pulling the curtain across the

windows as though the sight of the pattering rain against the glass irritated him. The pictures on the wall seemed to absorb him for a while, then even his own restlessness seemed to annoy him and he came to stand near to the girl who, with her eyes closed, finished drying her hair.

Even though she switched off the dryer, the high-pitched noise having made the ensuing silence seem loud, she did not open her eyes. There was in her pose no provocation nor invitation. She was lost in a world that no one could penetrate.

It was not until Todd Alexander spoke that she realized he was still there, that she was in unfamiliar territory, and that she had been sitting on his bed, shoulders rounded, her head hanging dejectedly.

For the second time that day he asked, "Something wrong?" It was then that she realized just where her dreaming had taken her—lying in Jasper's arms on her parents' couch in the living room of the apartment in which she lived.

It took a tremendous effort to rouse herself from the unhappiness that had gripped her, and make her eyes focus on reality instead of her dream. She shook her head slowly, then realized how much of her own self she was revealing and changed it, like a lightning flash, into a brilliant smile.

"Something wrong? No, of course not. Why should there be?"

A few moments later, the dryer was back in its box and being held out to him. "Thanks for asking for the use of this." He indicated that she should put it down on a table. "Well," she sighed, looking around as if reluctant to leave the luxury of her surroundings, "I must go home now. I do hope it's stopped raining, don't you?"

Alicia felt that her artificial smile must have set like a plaster cast, and that if she didn't revert to her own personality soon she would have to chip the smile away with a hammer and chisel.

"No, it has not stopped raining. Far from it." He lifted the receiver and Alicia heard him informing reception that the hair dryer could be picked up. He added, "I would like a table for two this evening. Seven-thirty. Yes, earlier than usual. Thanks."

Hurriedly, Alicia stood. "I'm sorry, Mr. Alexander. I'd no idea you had a dinner engagement." She picked up her handbag. He took it from her. Her brow pleated anxiously. "I can't get home without that, Mr. Alexander. It's got my money and my keys."

"*You* are my guest."

The frown turned to anger. He hadn't even asked. His high-handedness was needling her. Jasper's letter whispered, "Enjoys going out." And what else was waiting for her at home but Jasper's letter? The frown was banished. The smile was back. "Why, thank you, Mr. Alexander. It'll be great eating here, actually having all that wonderful food on the menu offered to me instead of just the menu hanging in front of my nose tantalizing me."

"It will be a pleasure having your company at the table." The pleasure he spoke of did not show in his eyes. Even his smile was devoid of sincerity. Was that how hers appeared to him? But she was better at acting than he was. It was plain that he had only invited her to dine with him out of politeness.

So maybe she had better give him a means of extricating himself from his strong sense of duty. "I've . . . I've just remembered, Mr. Alexander—I can't dine with you. It's very kind of you but I promised to meet a friend—''

"The table's booked. There's the phone. Call your friend and cancel."

He had called her bluff! Yet some pretense would have to be made, if only for the sake of her own pride. She lifted the receiver, hesitated, then replaced it. "My friend won't be there yet. Home from work, I mean." The plaster smile was back. "It was a very . . . well, elastic arrangement. If one of us didn't turn up, the other was to go . . . wherever they wanted to go."

Was he convinced by her little subterfuge? His maddeningly unreadable brown eyes gave nothing away. His curved mouth formed a smile, but whether it was cynical or sincere, she did not know enough about the man to decide.

"If I'm dining with you, I'll have to try and make myself presentable, so—"

"To me, you seem perfectly presentable."

"Presentable"—a nice, neutral word that meant exactly nothing—not "full of life," nor "great, just great." Just plain presentable. That was how a man—any man, it seemed, even Todd Alexander since it was his word—saw her. It was no good, she admonished herself, she would just *have* to stop torturing herself with Jasper's comments. All the same, they hurt, they still hurt.

The small smile she gave her host was too fragile to be anything but genuine. He seemed to be watching her closely, so closely it worried her. After the dinner he was going to pay for, would he expect "other things" of her? Would he assume that with her, like Jasper's new girl friend, "anything goes," too?

"I—I must tidy up." She swung around toward the bathroom—and something resting on the bedside cabinet caught her eye. It was a picture frame, in position and supported by its stand. There was something strange about it. It was empty! Alicia stared at it, seeing her own face reflected faintly in the glass.

The question was in her eyes as she looked at him and he answered softly, "I use it as a reminder, Miss Granger, of woman's faithlessness and inconstancy."

"You mean—" She stopped herself as she was about to tread on dangerous ground. "You mean there's been a woman in your life? One who meant so much to you you've condemned all others because she—"

His deepening frown stopped her and he said tersely, "Was playing around with one man while engaged to another."

"You were the one she was engaged to?"

"You seem surprised."

The tip of her tongue ran over her lips. The sudden return to customary aloofness was unnerving. "Well, yes, I—I just didn't associate you with . . . with . . . ." Would he rescue her by finishing the statement as he had done earlier? It seemed not. He lounged, eyes hooded, against the drawer extension of the dressing table, watching her flounder. "With enough depth of . . . of feeling to . . . well, love anyone."

Although the words had been spoken with honesty, they rang, even to her own ears, as a challenge. The recoil of her body was an entirely involuntary reaction to the threat in his eyes.

"I mean . . . ." She had to placate him, he was, after all, her host. "You've always held yourself so aloof. Even now, while I've been in here, you've been completely unbending in your attitude. That doesn't mean," she added hastily as he started advancing toward her, "that I'm not grateful for everything you've done, but—" She was backing away now. "But you're like a man encased in . . . in ice and— No, please, Mr. Alexander, I haven't been encouraging you. . . ."

His hands, on her upper arms, bit deep into her flesh.

"I was only speaking the truth, Mr. Alexander," she blurted out, wincing at the pain. "I mean, the truth as . . . as others see it. Not just me. The other girls . . . they say—"

Slowly, relentlessly, he was pulling her closer. "So now," he grated, "you'll be able to tell them differently, won't you?"

Even as the soft curves of her were compressed against him, she shook her head. "No, no, I didn't mean—"

"I know what you meant. This." The words came through his teeth, and then those teeth were grinding unmercifully against hers. His wide, sensual mouth was taking command of her lips, parting them and discovering that the taste was greatly to his liking. At first resisting with all her energies, her resistance broke as the vibrations arising from the essential maleness of the body against hers penetrated her barriers, activated her arms and linked them around his neck.

When he let her go it was with roughness and a curious anger. Her instinct was to shout at him that she was not that kind of girl, that his right to kiss her had been less than nil—then she remembered Jasper's tormenting words. She "enjoys going out. Other things, too. . . ."

The strangled breathing that was making her lungs fight for air calmed to normal at last and she fixed the plaster smile back into place. *I'm a bundle of fun, remember*, she admonished herself, *living life to the full*.

Her smile was dazzling. "That . . . that was great, Mr. Alexander." His icy gaze was frightening after such a show of passion, cold and meaningless though it was. Her smile did not falter. "I'll be able to tell the girls how—" again she moistened her lips "—how warmhearted you really are." She had been backing toward the bathroom. Feeling the door with her hands, she turned into the sanctuary of its tiled neutrality and turned the key.

"THERE WAS NO NEED for you to arrange for me to dine with you." Alicia spoke to Todd Alexander over the top of her menu. He continued to study his copy. "If you think so little of women," she continued with her verbal prodding, "I can't understand why you chose to burden your private hours with one of them, especially me."

As he put his menu down, his smile was hard. "To be truthful, Miss Granger, neither can I. Maybe—" he moved the menu so that it ran exactly parallel to his place setting "—maybe it was in payment for that kiss you gave me."

"But you ordered dinner for two before you—we— Anyway, you took the kiss from me. I didn't give it voluntarily."

He leaned back, regarding her, the light in his eyes belying the coldness of his outward bearing. "At first you might have been a little reluctant, but halfway through you changed your mind. I remember I had to disengage myself from you." It was a taunt and it went home. Her scarlet cheeks seemed to amuse him.

"It was involuntary," she snapped. "You see, *I'm a*

normal, warmhearted human being and if my responses
follow my feminine instincts, can I help it?"

"Are you provoking me again?" He appeared to have
it in mind to push back his chair and come around to her.

I wouldn't put it past him, she thought, *to behave like
primitive man and drag me by the hair up to his room
again.* "Primitive man." The words excited and disturbed,
stirring unfamiliar feelings. Firmly, she quietened them.

"No, no, Mr. Alexander." Her artificial smile was back
in place. "Of *course* I wasn't provoking—any more than
I was last time."

He settled, unconvinced, back into his seat and the waiter
came to take the order. Todd asked Alicia for her choice
and, with no hesitation, she rattled off the names of the
dishes she had seen while studying the menu in the rain
outside the hotel. In spite of himself, Todd smiled. "Did
you get that?" he said to the waiter. The man nodded,
smiling while scribbling, then took Todd's order.

"Your French accent needs polishing," Todd commented when they were alone, "but your meaning came
over clearly. I gather you've discovered your appetite
now?"

"I'm starving," she replied, "up to here." Her hand
touched her chin. "Standing out there in the rain, this place
was like a—like a sanctuary. Somehow it was beckoning
me, but my bank balance said 'no.'"

"You couldn't have found a better place to linger outside," he said dryly. "Did you know I was staying here?
Had you heard?"

Her smile slipped out of sight. "That's the second time
you've insulted me this evening, Mr. Alexander. You now
seem to be implying that I waited outside knowing you'd

see me and invite me in. Well, you're wrong, *wrong*! If I'd known you were living here, I'd have gone the other way."

"When," he asked blandly, filling her glass with water and then his own, "was the first time?"

She frowned. "First time?"

"First insult," he prompted.

Taking a drink of water, she answered, "The kiss."

"Oh." He smiled. "So that was an insult. I've heard a kiss described by women in many ways, but never as an insult. At least the 'insulter' enjoyed it."

If the wine waiter had not appeared, Alicia knew that her bitter self would have lashed out at him. Todd asked for her preference where wine was concerned but she shook her head. "I have nothing to celebrate, thank you." Her voice had contained a nuance of bitterness, despite her efforts to eliminate it.

Her host looked at her, paused, handed back the wine list and dismissed the waiter. The moment she caught Todd watching her, she operated her brightness switch and simulated a bubbling vitality. "It's just great to be entertained to dinner this way. And by you, my boss. It's never happened to me before, not in any of the jobs I've worked in. To think I'd hardly spoken to you before this evening, too." Although she saw the quizzical expression on his face, it made no difference to her flow of words.

If being effervescent and vivacious and "full of life" aroused and kept a man's interest, then she would be all those things. Even the arrival of the food did not stem her flow of words. "Do you have any hobbies, Mr. Alexander?" She did not wait for an answer. "I've got dozens."

Her eyes watched the movement of the waiter's hands, but her tongue rattled on. "Not really passive ones, you understand, but things like—well, going out, and . . . er, dancing. And . . . and other things, too.''

She was lying blatantly, quoting as she was from Jasper's letter. But, she congratulated herself, she was lying convincingly—she could tell by the raised eyebrows of her host. The action was registering surprise, not disbelief, she was certain of that.

''This—'' she indicated the fast diminishing contents of her dish ''—this seafood something—''

''*Rémoulade*, meaning a sharp sauce,'' her host put in.

''Oh, yes, well, it's delicious. I honestly didn't know I was so hungry, Mr. Alexander.'' The food was almost choking her, but the taste was so good its effect on her was certainly not the fault of the chef. Jasper's words were still sticking in her throat, threatening an erruption of tears should she falter just once in her assumed role of prattling, animated guest.

There was a pause between courses and even that Alicia filled with a credible sigh of satisfaction, and a mimed and rapt interest in her surroundings. To her relief the second course quickly followed, and as she ate her way through it, she began to wish Todd Alexander were a more communicative host. Surely it was the custom of men to chat to their women guests? When Jasper took her anywhere— she corrected herself, had taken her anywhere—he had talked nonstop. They had laughed a lot, held hands—but where had it got them? To a letter from him, blunt, uncaring of hurt feelings. ''I've found another girl friend. . . .''

''Isn't the food to your liking this time?''

The question jerked her back to the glittering chandeliers, the dessert cart laden with mouth-watering offerings rolling past, the laughter of others.

It mustn't happen again, she told herself, that regression into the more serious personality that nature had given her.

"It's wonderful, Mr. Alexander," she responded to his question, eyes sparkling as if she had drunk champagne instead of water. "I only hope there's room for one of those mouth-watering desserts I watched go past a minute ago."

He smiled. "Since the treat's on me, Miss Granger, it would be a terrible pity, wouldn't it, if there wasn't."

Alicia managed to consume only half of the enticing piece of *gâteau* she had chosen from the cart. With a convincing appearance of regret, she put down her fork and sighed. "I knew I wouldn't make it," she said, her smile a mere shadow now.

All evening she had been wondering how long she would be able to keep up the pretense of possessing a personality that was the complete antithesis of the one with which she had been born. Now she sensed that the time had almost run out on her.

It was over coffee that her eyes began to play tricks. In the corner that they occupied, she was sure the lights had been lowered—or was it fatigue that made her eyelids droop and close? And when they fluttered open, was it the lurking shadows, her tiredness or wishful thinking that put Jasper across the table from her?

Holding her half-filled coffee cup, she stared—yes, it *was* Jasper staring back at her. He wasn't laughing as he used to do. There just wasn't any recognizable expression on his face. If he looked at her in such a way, it could only mean that he didn't love her anymore.

Her lips parted to ask him, "What's wrong with me? Do you dislike me now because I'm too serious? All right, so I'm not willing to indulge in the 'other things' you wrote about. So I'm unusual in wanting love to sweeten the act of loving. Take love away and what have you got—a selfish, meaningless interchange of nothing.''

Her eyelids, closing, encountered welling tears. Someone was taking her cup from her trembling hold. Her cheeks were damp and her face found a hiding place behind her outspread hands. "I'm sorry," she heard herself say. "I've spoiled your evening, I know I have. It was kind of you to wine and dine me, but—"

"No wine," the deep, tolerant voice corrected her. "Come on."

"My face, Mr. Alexander, I must dry my—"

"No one's looking. They're too busy eating. Here." A handkerchief was pushed into her hand. "Mop up while I settle the bill."

Her coat was being slipped onto her arms and shoulders, a hand was under her elbow guiding her. A few moments waiting in the warmth of the hotel foyer then a doorman came and said, "Your car's here, Mr. Alexander."

His car? Alicia emerged from the daze that had enveloped her from the moment she had "seen" Jasper. "It's too far to drive, Mr. Alexander," she said agitatedly. "Just give me a lift to the nearest subway station and I'll—"

"You'll get in my car." He preceded her through the swing door, pulling her after him. "Just tell me where." He spoke in a voice that demanded an answer.

"North of London." She named the town, then tried again. "There's no need to take me."

They were the last words spoken for some time. All Todd's attention was on the traffic although this, as they moved at last from London's environs, grew lighter. Sensing Todd's limbs and muscles relaxing beside her, Alicia relaxed, too. The seat's cushioned headrest was kind to her aching head and she closed her eyes.

It seemed a few moments later that she heard a voice prodding her to wakefulness. The car was still, but only a few houses were to be seen. They appeared to be parked in a service road alongside the main road. A dog was barking, objecting to their presence but the inhabitants of the houses seemed to prefer the coziness of their living rooms to the damp, dark evening outside.

"We're there," Todd Alexander was saying. "You must tell me the road and the number of your house."

Apologizing, Alicia sat up, but a hand pushed her back. "Who's Jasper?" Todd asked.

CHAPTER TWO

"HOW DO YOU KNOW about Jasper?" The question was a horrified whisper.

In the semidarkness his face was angled and shadowed. She could not see his eyes. He was leaning over her, finding her eyes easily as the street lamps caught them. "You told me about him as we drank our coffee."

"No, I couldn't," There was panic in her voice, "I was thinking. You couldn't hear my thoughts."

"You were thinking aloud. You asked me what was wrong with you and if I disliked you because you were a serious person. You said you didn't like the loving without the love."

"Oh, God." Her hand covered her face again, "I didn't mean you to hear. It was Jasper I was talking to. I could see him sitting where you were. . . . "

"Three times I've seen you cry tonight. Once in the office, once outside the hotel—"

She shook her head vigorously. "It was the rain, not tears."

"When I see something with my own eyes, I believe my eyes. There were tears for the third time with the coffee. Tonight has been an extraordinary experience. I've never entertained two women to dinner before, two women in one. One had a plastic smile and eyes that looked as though grannules of artificial glitter had been sprinkled in them.

She bubbled and babbled and danced to an inaudible tune as if some unseen person had wound her up. She drooped and drifted away, came back, but was no happier. The other had a mouth that trembled and eyes like a cloud-covered sky. There was a third lurking somewhere, but we won't go into that now." A finger flicked a curl that had strayed over her cheek. "Which of them was the real you, my friend?"

His friend? Somehow the word made her feel worse, yet she could not understand why. "The second," she said fiercely. "The drooping, drifting, miserable one. The one who was full of seriousness, not life, who doesn't love dancing or going out or—" She was crying again, and there was absolutely nothing she could do about it.

The handkerchief appeared again, but she pushed it away. Then her cheek was against a man's jacket, feeling the hard chest beneath, hearing between her sobs a drumming beat. Strong arms held her, offering comfort and solace. Sympathy and understanding, too, as he said, "Jasper's a boyfriend. Am I right?"

"Past tense," she mumbled, her hands pressed against his diaphragm, feeling it expand and contract.

"He's found another girl." She nodded against him, finding in his strength and solidity a strange, tear-drying comfort. "He called you— No. Wrote to you? Yes. Told you how lovely she is, how animated and overflowing with life she is—and how often she says 'yes' in comparison with your 'no.' "

"You must be a mind reader after all," she muttered.

"If I am, it could be because I'm familiar with the situation myself. Remember?"

Her breathing held momentarily. It was true, their situations were similar. "But you're a man. You can take the emotional knocks better than a woman."

A hand stroked and rested against her hair. "You must be joking." Her head shook negatively against him. "Then your statement reveals how little you know of mankind compared to womankind."

"Yes, but—" She pushed away a little to dab at her eyes and cheeks. "Look at you with your picture frame. You told me you've stopped trusting women. I haven't stopped trusting men. For instance, I would *never* mistrust a man with your integrity."

The comforting, stroking hand stilled.

"Even if," she added, "you did kiss me so . . . so horribly earlier this evening."

"I didn't notice your repulsing me," he responded dryly. "I remember I had to force your arms from around my neck—"

She pulled away and he let her go. "Why are you so bitter, Mr. Alexander?"

"Maybe—" he straightened his tie and rebuttoned his jacket "—it's because a man doesn't cry like a woman. Maybe it's a man's only means of retaliation against those 'emotional knocks' you talked about."

A fit of shivering took her by surprise and she yawned deeply. "I'm sorry, Mr. Alexander. It's been a long day. It started with a letter of rejection from a man I—" She reconsidered. "I thought I loved." Odd that, she thought, I really did think I loved him. "And it ended—" a watery smile was turned to him in the lamplight "—dining with the boss." She peered at the clock on the dashboard. "Just look at the time, Mr. Alexander. And you've got a long

way to go.'' She told him her apartment was not far away
and directed him to it.

Pulling up outside, he got out and walked around to
Alicia's door. As she collected her wits and her belongings,
she said, ''Thank you for this evening. You've been very
kind and understanding. I—''

It seemed as if he had been only half listening. He turned
from scrutinizing the apartment block and said, ''A cup of
coffee would be welcome before I start my journey back.''

Coloring at her own impoliteness, she stammered, ''Of—
of course. I should have asked you. Please come in.'' He
followed and she said, ''First floor, left-hand side. The
ground-floor apartment on the left is for sale.''

Taking out her key, her hand shook as she unlocked.
Was he *that* kind after all? Was he expecting the ''other
things'' Jasper had talked about in his letter?

He was, at that moment, more interested in the apartment.
With relief she saw his gaze wander and his eyes grow
reflective, not about what he might be expecting of her, but
at the obvious good taste of the furnishings, the air of
quality, the touch of affluence.

Then he did look at her, eyebrows raised in a faintly
cynical question. ''You have a comfortable little nest to
live in, Miss Granger.''

It took no more than a few seconds for her to catch up
with his train of thought. Angrily she responded, ''What
are you thinking, Mr. Alexander? That my ex-boyfriend—
for 'boyfriend' read 'lover'—did me proud by buying me
this apartment? Are you wondering just how much I did to
please him to merit such a 'comfortable little nest'?''

She threw her bag onto a chair, peeled off her coat and
dropped it to the floor. ''You know what, Mr. Alexander?

Your mistrust of womankind, just because you were let down by your fiancée, sickens me.''

He stood, hands in pockets, watching and listening.

''Shall I show you a picture of my 'lover,' Mr. Alexander?'' She went into her bedroom and emerged with a picture in a frame. ''There he is, there's Jasper. Doesn't he look rich and elegant and cigar-smoking and fat?''

Thrusting the picture into Todd's hands she pointed to the young, smiling face, the carefully pointed beard, the eyes that reflected a youthful zest for living. ''Look carefully and you might see his worn shirt collar. If it wasn't only a head and shoulders portrait, you'd see the holes in the sweater's elbows, the faded jeans and the blue-and-white running shoes on his feet.''

Snatching the picture from Todd's hands, she hurled it to the floor, bent down and poked her fingers through the broken glass. In pulling the photograph from the smashed frame she cut her fingers, but she disregarded the blood. With a vicious movement she tore the picture to pieces and threw it away.

''Now, *now* I've got it out of my system—him, his nasty innuendos about my character; boyfriends, men in general.'' She looked around for something to stem the flow of blood and seized a tissue from a box, wrapping it around and pressing it to the wound. ''I won't spend my life being bitter, like you. I won't condemn all men as you've condemned all women.'' Breathing deeply she stared at her guest, waiting for his reaction.

For a few moments he let her simmer, then asked tonelessly, ''Are you feeling better now you've spilled your blood in a curious form of primitive sacrifice? Are your mind and body cured of the torment that seems to have afflicted them ever since that letter arrived this morning?"

The throbbing pain of the cuts was coming through, bringing with it a feeling of annoyance at the impetuosity that had brought about the self-inflicted wounds.

"Or," he continued, "do you intend to go on abusing me for an insinuation I never made?"

"I'm sorry," she said at last, emerging from the numbness that had swept over her since her outburst. "Today I've been through a kind of personal hell." She looked down at her hands. "I can't stop the bleeding."

He inspected the cuts and frowned. "They must be washed and covered with a dressing. Where're the bandages?"

"In the bathroom."

He followed her, saying, "Since it's your right hand that's been hurt, I'll attend to it."

He washed his hands over the bathtub while she went to the sink and ran cold water over the cuts, cleansing them. As he dressed the wounds, Alicia looked up into his face, liking the thick dark eyebrows that matched his hair, the straight nose, the well-marked cheekbones.

He looked up from tending her fingers and caught her scrutiny. His mouth, which had savaged hers in his hotel bedroom earlier that evening, softened into a smile. Or was it not a softening at all, but that cynicism that had so angered her just now and prompted her explosive display of temper?

Embarrassed at being caught examining his features she said quickly, "Did you really think this was my boyfriend's apartment? Or that he was paying the rent for me?"

His smile persisted but it gave nothing away. "I was

thinking exactly what I said, that it was a comfortable place to live in.''

''You didn't say that exactly. You said—''

''Never mind what I said. Is the place yours?''

''It belongs to my parents. There are two bedrooms. My parents are abroad in connection with my father's job, so I'm living here alone.''

''Which explains the expensive air of the place. I couldn't understand how a mere working girl could afford such things.''

''So that 'mere working girl' just had to have a man behind the scenes paying for the place—or sharing it with her.''

His work was done and he washed his hands again. ''That's the way of it these days, isn't it?'' He dried his hands on the towel she gave him. ''Live together, make love together, maybe even go through a ceremony and sign a register. Later, maybe a year, maybe two—'' he handed back the towel ''—comes the parting and the divorce.''

''You're a cynic right throught to the marrow in your bones,'' she accused.

He laughed briefly, then shrugged. ''I'm a realist. Don't confuse the two. Anyway, if I am a cynic, does it matter? I've had my fill of women. I've vowed never to marry. But if any woman at any time offers me the benefits of marriage without the ceremony, I'll take it—and her—with open arms.''

Alicia turned away. His words upset her. Was it because they reminded her only too vividly of the casualness of Jasper's abandonment of her for another girl? As she made the coffee, she sensed Todd was watching her but she would not look around. Then he was close behind her, his hands closing on her shoulders.

"We're two of a kind, Alicia," he stated, his voice warmer than she had heard it before. "I've been through that same hell and recovered, and I can guarantee you'll recover, too."

He turned her face to him and for a few seconds, she battled with her tears. Smiling through them into his blurring face, she whispered, "This time I can see you, not Jasper."

"That," he said, his eyes wandering over her mouth, "is at least a step in the right direction."

The kiss his eyes had considered came at last, tender, gentle and full of promise. For some reason that escaped her comprehension, since she had been so sure she loved Jasper, she experienced an intense feeling of elation. But her inner self warned that the promise Todd's kiss had contained would never be fulfilled.

IT WAS WITH PART EXCITEMENT, part dread that Alicia entered the office next morning. How would Todd Alexander react when he saw her?

When his fellow director, Halmar Seagar, came into the office and informed her that Mr. Alexander would be away all day on business, she could not account for the way her heart seemed to sway like a circus performer on a tightrope.

"Are my letters ready, Miss Granger?" Mr. Seager asked benignly.

"All here for your signature," she answered, watching him write his name with a flourish. If only he knew the string of events to which those letters had led! In a way, she supposed she should thank him for being the cause of her dining with the boss, not to mention all the other things!

The man's mind was already busy with the meeting he was attending at a company along London's Embankment. "I came in early and dictated another batch of letters," he told her, packing his briefcase and fastening it securely. "If you finish those, you'll find a couple of handwritten reports to be typed in the top drawer of the locked filing cabinet in my office. Er—" He paused at the door and, as others had drifted in and what he had to say seemed confidential, he returned to stand by her desk.

Putting up his hand and speaking behind it—thus, Alicia thought with amusement, drawing even more attention to himself—he said, "The key to the cabinet is locked in my desk drawer. Here's the key to that. Take care that no one except Mr. Alexander sees those reports. They are extremely confidential. Can I trust you not to reveal them to anyone, nor to say a single word about their contents to anybody else, with the exception of Mr. Alexander?"

His voice had been low and the others had, fortunately, soon lost interest in Mr. Seagar's melodramatic gesture. Alicia nodded, her curiosity aroused. When he had gone, she frowned at the responsibility that had so unexpectedly been laid at her door.

"Good morning, Alicia." Leonard Richardson appeared beside her. His desk was across the aisle and two or three to the rear of Alicia's. She looked up at him after uncovering her typewriter.

His hair was short and of an indefinable brown color. His unfashionable suit had seen a few years' wear and hung on him as if he had lost weight. His features were regular, his manner quiet. His voice matched his manner, his smile like that of someone who never expected one in return. Often Alicia lunched with him, always at a small café nearby. He was an undemanding companion and Alicia found it almost a relaxation to eat with him in the impersonal surroundings of the café, rather than with the others in the slightly rowdy, noisily friendly atmosphere of the local pub.

"Hi, Leonard." Part of her was sorry for Leonard. He seemed a lonely person, rarely at ease even with the other men employees.

"Eating with the others today?" he asked. The note of hope was there, intermingled with a touch of resignation should the answer be "yes."

"Tell you later," she answered, hoping he would leave her so that she could get on with her work. He stood indecisively for a moment, then went on his way.

It took Alicia until lunchtime to finish the letters that Mr. Seager had dictated into the machine. Having in mind the man's warning about the confidential reports that were awaiting typing, she covered the finished letters with a folder, deciding that she would type their envelopes on her return from lunch.

In the café, conversation with Leonard was threatening to lag.

"You spend so much time on your own," she admonished, "you've forgotten how to talk to your fellow human beings."

He smiled uncomfortably. "I'm a lonely person, hadn't you noticed? I don't join in, which means that others don't join me."

"Except me." She smiled, attempting to provoke a smile back. Momentarily, the corners of his mouth lifted, but not for long.

"Feeling sorry for yourself today?" she teased. Living alone as he did, Alicia guessed that she was the only person he could talk to.

"You would be, if you found yourself in a job that was way below your real abilities." His sudden vehemence surprised her, "Why have I been put onto a routine job that anyone could do with just a basic knowledge of engineering, when I've got a good honors degree? I'm a designer, not an odd-job man messing around with sketching diagrams of components and the nuts and bolts of car mechanics."

He edged forward and spoke with a suppressed excitement.

"They're onto something, Alicia. I could sense it from the way Mr. Scager was whispering to you this morning. I heard him talk about a report to be typed."

Alicia's eyes widened. So Mr. Seager had been overheard! She had been concentrating so much on listening to him, she had not noticed anything else. As Mr. Seager had stooped over her desk, Leonard must have been near enough to hear the director's whispered words.

"It's confidential, Leonard," she said and stood up to go.

On the way back to the office, Alicia had spoken only a little. How, she was wondering, could she type those reports without Leonard seeing them? Even when she reached her desk, she had not solved the problem. As she put the letters in a pile, with the envelope flaps overlapping the top of each letter, and prepared to take them to Mr. Seager's office, she was still wondering.

Raking in her handbag, she extracted a powder compact. Lifting it high, she pretended to inspect her face. Through the reflection of the compact's mirror, she could see that

Leonard was looking at her. When he lost interest, she closed the compact quietly and slipped it back into her bag, her fingers feeling for and bringing out in her closed hand, the key to Mr. Seager's desk.

Taking up the pile of letters, she walked toward the door, stopping to chat for a few moments to a friend. Then she went out into the corridor and made for Mr. Seager's office. Once inside, she closed the door, wishing there had been a key to turn. For some reason, she felt afraid. Why had she been given the confidential work to do? She knew the answer—it was because the secretary who worked for both Todd Alexander and Mr. Seagar had left the day before, prior to having a baby.

Placing the letters for signature on Mr. Seagar's desk, she unlocked the the top drawer and took out the key to the filing cabinet. This she opened, pulling out the top drawer. The reports were there as Mr. Seagar had said. Looking around the room, she wished Mr. Seagar had a spare desk and typewriter in there just like the one in the head of the company's office.

That was the answer! Todd was out for the day, so why couldn't she use the typewriter in his room? Even looking at the communicating door between the offices was daunting. Slowly, she eased it open. It was a large room and it was empty. Closing the door, she tiptoed to the desk in the corner, as if afraid of waking someone sleeping in the boss's chair.

The idea made her smile, but it soon passed when she realized she had no typing paper. It wouldn't be possible, she decided, to return to the general office and leave it again immediately without arousing Leonard's suspicions. The only solution was to search in Todd's room for the paper.

From experience she knew that there was a stack of paper in a cupboard. If it was the right size, then she would help herself and hope he would never notice.

It was the correct size and she extracted a number of sheets. It was only when she was well into the second page that she began to realize the significance of the handwritten reports she had been given to type. Her fingers slowed and stopped and her eyes continued to read.

There were sketches and diagrams and technical terms that were far beyond her understanding. Yet somehow she guessed that it was a report of research carried out by a company called Sander Design of a car that seemed to be called the Lone Ranger.

There was a reference to an approaching breakthrough in the design of a new type of battery that powered the electric car, lengthening its range before renewal of its power source was necessary. If the design succeeded, the report went on, it would be possible to give the vehicle a higher top speed, plus other refinements.

The name of the company puzzled her, until it came to her how it must have been formed—from the last two syllables of the name Alexander. Having finished the report she was flicking back to where she had stopped typing when the door behind her opened. Her first thought was that Leonard had come to seek her out.

"No, Leonard," she shouted, trying with her hands and arms to cover the typewritten sheets and hoping that her voice would penetrate to the corridor. "You can't."

"Can't I?" Alicia swung around to meet the furious eyes of the head of the company. The door slammed behind him and Alicia stammered, "M-Mr. Seagar said you'd gone out for the day, so—"

"Who gave you permission to work in my room?" He had moved nearer and the ice in his eyes had numbed her heart with frostbite. It wouldn't take much, she warned herself, for that arm to lift, for his finger to point to the door—and to instant dismissal from the firm. Her explanation would have to be good, but even when she had told him the truth, would he believe her?

"Nobody, Mr. Alexander." She was standing now, twisting a pencil between her fingers.

His hands found his hips beneath his jacket. "So, on the basis of one evening spent together, you walked in as calmly as if you owned the place, and clinched, all by yourself, a takeover bid for my office."

"Last night had nothing to do with it," she protested, although her own heart whispered otherwise. "These reports—" She gestured toward the typewriter. "Mr. Seagar gave me to understand that they were very confidential—"

"Which they are," he interrupted curtly.

"And also," she continued, "that I mustn't let anyone see them, except you. I . . . ." She put the pencil down and rubbed her moist palms together. "I was so afraid that . . . that—" It was no use, she could not bring herself to mention Leonard's interest, having no wish to say anything that might lose him his job.

"You were afraid—" Todd reminded her, his eyebrows raised.

"Afraid that, while I typed them, someone—anyone—might come and speak to me and I might forget to hide the sheets, and anyway, if I did, it would let them know I *had* something to hide, which would only arouse their suspicions and—"

"Message received and decoded, Miss Granger." Todd walked to his own desk near the window. "All that remains to be explained is why you chose to work in my office and not Mr. Seagar's."

The answer to that was so easy she smiled. "There isn't a typewriter in Mr. Seagar's room."

"You can take that plastic smile off your face. It was bad enough last night dining with two women. I refuse to be made to put up with the presence of two typists in my office while I work."

"So you don't mind my working in here?"

"In the circumstances," he responded with a long-suffering sigh, "it would be all the same if I did, wouldn't it? By the way, how are your injuries?"

She held up her hands. "The left one's okay. The right is still sore. But," she added hastily, "it doesn't affect my ability to type."

"Don't state the obvious," he commented, easing into his seat and looking pointedly at the typewritten sheets on her desk.

She took the hint with bad grace. All right, so he disliked women, but why, she wondered as she worked, include her? What harm had she ever done him? Then she remembered the empty picture frame in his hotel bedroom and knew that, if she entertained any secret hopes of his changing his mind about womankind, then she might as well wish that all the stars were diamonds and that they all belonged to her.

CHAPTER THREE

WHEN ALICIA FINISHED TYPING the reports, it was time to go home. Todd was still at his desk. Now and then the telephone had rung and her instinct had been to hurry across and answer it. Each time his hand on the receiver had forestalled her.

At last he had said, "There's no doubt you were successfully indoctrinated with the secretary mentality at the college where you learned your office skills." He was smiling, but as usual, it stopped short of his eyes. "Protect your boss at all costs, dance to his tune, run at his bidding, run even when he doesn't bid, since a good secretary should anticipate her boss's needs."

Alicia laughed. "His *every* need, Mr. Alexander?" Her eyebrows were arched in mock innocence.

"Are you flirting with me?" One of his eyebrows flicked up.

"Never, Mr. Alexander! I know my place." Her grin was mischievous and provocative.

"Do you, indeed? Tell me," he capped his gold pen and pocketed it, "where would that be?"

"Why, right here in the typist's chair, Mr. Alexander. Where else did you think I meant?"

He half rose, his eyes crossing the space between them, even though his legs did not. Then he subsided into his seat. Through heavy-lidded eyes, he looked at her and said,

"Come to my hotel room tonight, Miss Granger, and I'll not only tell you, I'll put you there."

Her laughter filled the room, and he watched her dancing eyes.

"Are you going to ask me which Alicia Granger I am now, Mr. Alexander?" she ventured, wondering how far she could go with him. "Am I the babbling, bubbling one, or the drooping, drifting one?"

Yes, he had recalled his definitions of the evening before. His smile was enigmatic. "Neither. And I never ask a question to which I already know the answer." There was the sound of chattering in the corridor. The other employees were going home.

"The reports are finished, Mr. Alexander. Shall I replace them in Mr. Seagar's filing cabinet, lock it and place the key in his desk, locking that, then give you the key?"

He rubbed the area between his brows. "You're forcing my tired brain to work overtime," he said with sarcasm. "Simplify the whole matter by giving me the reports and the key. I'll see to the rest." As he took the neat piles of paper, he said, "My friend and colleague, Halmar Seagar, seems to have placed an enormous amount of trust in you. You realize—" now his eyes, as they caught hers, were hard and businesslike "—that this is the company's top secret? It's a project known only to myself and Halmar, plus the very gifted young scientists we have working on the problem. And now you. I hope Halmar's faith in your discretion and honesty are justified?"

Alicia was angry that, by his questioning of his colleague's action in taking her into their confidence, he was revealing his own doubts about her. "My integrity is as good as yours, Mr. Alexander."

Her eyes were not dancing now. They were fighting, challenging—and hurt. "Why don't you have a security check carried out on me?" she persisted. "They'd be wasting their time because I live a plain and honest life. No intrigues, no secret love affairs, no bugging devices up my sleeves." She tugged at the wrist-fastening cuffs of her white shirt-blouse.

"Okay, Miss Granger, my friend." His eyes were mocking as they noted the slight wince she gave at his dispassionate placing of her in his scale of associates. "I understand the message you're putting across. But—" He rose and swung around the desk, confronting her. "Heaven help you—" his hands cupped her face, forcing back her head, gripping her until it hurt "—if you ever betray the trust Halmar Seagar and I have placed in you. You do understand?"

She tried to nod but his hold was so tight she could only whisper, "Yes."

The pressure of his hands on her cheeks formed her lips into an inviting pout. He did not even try to resist the invitation. His mouth came down, slowly, slowly, until her eyes widened with her mounting desire for his kiss.

As it came, her eyes closed and she abandoned herself to the rising current of feeling, which had turned from a rippling stream to a roaring river in a few seconds. Her hands found his arms to pull at them to release her. Instead, she found her own arms creeping to his neck and crossing there as if to prevent his pulling away. There were tears in her eyes from the pain his hands were inflicting on her cheeks, but they just seemed to add to the pleasure of his kiss.

When he let her go, she staggered back, finding the desk to rest against.

His breathing had quickened a little, but that was all. Had the man's feeling gone completely dead? Did she really leave him as cold as he appeared?

"For someone who spent most of yesterday weeping over her lost love," he drawled, "you've just given a very impressive imitation of a woman who has recovered from heartbreak in record time."

"Maybe," she fought back, "I pretended you were Jasper."

"Did you?"

She evaded the question with another question. "Why did you do it?" Somehow she could not rid herself of a sense of humiliation, although she could not find a reason for it. Was it because of the way he reacted—as if she was to him, just another woman, her lips just another pair of lips to kiss?

He returned to his seat but did not sit down. He flicked through the reports she had handed over. "To seal the bargain we made."

"There wasn't a—"

He looked up quickly. "There was."

It was true, there was a bargain between them. He had forced the acquiescence from her, barbarically, but effectively. "You do understand?" He spoke coldly and insistently. "Tell me again you understand that you must treat this matter—" he tapped the reports "—with the utmost secrecy."

"I understand." Unaccountably, her voice, like her spirits, had dropped. Slowly she walked to the typist's desk, picked up her handbag and went to the door.

"She's back, the droopy one."

Alicia turned and caught him smiling. "She's the proper one," she answered wearily. "The bright one's just one big bluff."

"So who was the girl in my arms?"

"Someone I didn't even know myself," she answered and went out.

"WHERE DID YOU GET TO yesterday afternoon?"

Leonard was standing at Alicia's desk next morning when she arrived. His mood was that of a jealous boyfriend, which annoyed her. He had no claim on her except that of friendship and even that was only during working hours.

"I—er—wanted some peace, so I found another office. An empty one," she added, hoping to distract his attention from the subject. "I needed some peace and quiet," she elaborated. At his surprised look and fearing deeper questioning that might cause her to reveal the secret with which she had been entrusted, she confessed, "The day before yesterday I got a letter from my boyfriend. My *ex*-boyfriend," she added bitterly. "He told me he'd found another girl, someone who—" Even now it hurt to think about it. "Pleased him better. In every way. I'm—just not that sort."

"I guessed that," Leonard said with surprising sincerity. "And I'm sorry to know you've been upset by personal events."

He had been successfully sidetracked, Alicia thought, but she'd meant every bit of the bitterness she had implied. As she removed her typewriter cover, Leonard was still beside her. "What happened?" he asked, pointing to the plasters on her fingers.

"Oh, those. They were there yesterday. I cut my hand.

On a picture frame. Well—'' she sat down, smoothing her skirt ''—to be truthful, on the glass of the frame. I smashed my ex-boyfriend's picture, then tore him up.''

"Cutting your hands on the glass?"

She forced a smile, her "plastic" one, as Todd would have called it. "Leonard Richardson, private detective."

"There's no need to be sarcastic,'' he said, looking hurt, "even if your boyfriend has gone off with someone else. Anyway. . . .'' There was his hopeful smile again. "There's always me.''

"That's kind of you, Leonard. Next time it'll be your shoulder I'll cry on.''

"Why?" he asked suspiciously. "Whose shoulder was it first?''

"My goodness, you're quick,'' she commented, putting on her smile, but secretly startled by the way he picked up the slightest clue. "Anyway, why should I tell you my secrets?''

"When you've finished your conversation, Miss Granger,'' the clipped voice came from the door, "I should like to see you in my office.''

Alicia's cheeks turned a deep pink. "Yes, Mr. Alexander,'' she replied as he withdrew from the room.

"Now I know who it was,'' Leonard said thoughtfully, noting the blush.

"Knew who what was?'' Alicia parried, annoyed that her face gave away her feelings with such speed and accuracy.

Smoothing her hair, she made for the door, leaving Leonard looking at her retreating figure.

Gazing at Todd Alexander across his desk was like coming face to face with an iceberg. "I don't like office gossip," he said, pushing a hand into his pocket. "It wastes the firm's time. Also, when one of the persons involved in it has been entrusted with confidential information, it could lead to misunderstandings. You get me?" His eyes couldn't, Alicia decided, turn any colder.

"I understand you perfectly, Mr. Alexander."

"Good. Now I'll tell you what I wanted you for. From today, you will be working here in my office. That way—" his eyes swept over her as he looked up from arranging the pens on the desk "—I can keep you under surveillance."

Her heart beat a little faster as she tried and failed to guess his meaning. "No office gossip, Mr. Alexander?" Her eyes dared his as he stood facing her. "No unguarded tongue spilling top secrets to anyone and everyone?"

He came around the desk, his head down a little. "No unguarded tongue being cheeky to the boss."

Involuntarily, Alicia backed away. "I didn't mean to be."

"I have to contradict you." He really did look angry. "You had every intention."

There was no answer to his statement, since he was right. "When do I move in?" she asked, succeeding in taking the heat out of the situation.

"Now. Use the desk and typewriter over there that you used yesterday. An extension desk will be brought in."

"Could I have a filing cabinet, please?" She had made her tone so polite that even he could not criticize it.

"Put in a requisition for one. No, make that two."

"Yes, Mr. Alexander."

He scutinized her face for impudence, but found only her expressionless blue eyes looking at him.

When she returned with her belongings, Todd Alexander

had gone. There was a note on her desk. "As from today, you are promoted to being my personal assistant. Your salary will increase accordingly. A telephone extension will be installed for your use. All calls to me will be channeled through you. That way, our hands won't collide in reaching for my own telephone." Alicia could almost see his sardonic smile. The note continued, "I shall be out for most of the day. If you finish the letters on the machine, Halmar Seagar will give you work. He will also know where to contact me, should the need arise. T.A."

Promotion, personal assistant, higher salary? Alicia felt the need for a seat. What would it be like working every day in close proximity to the man with a power of personality, not to mention a personal magnetism, so strong that to resist being drawn into his sphere of influence was like fighting against a hundred-mile-an-hour blizzard in the Arctic!

Alicia spent the morning typing the dictated letters, making the most of the peace and quiet that prevailed in the office without Todd's disturbing presence. At lunchtime, she made her way back to the general office, only to be surrounded by envious girls, who until that morning, were her equals in status.

"Yes, it's true," she answered their questions, "but I certainly don't feel like a personal assistant, not to anyone, let alone the boss!"

On the edge of the crowd, Leonard hovered. When the others had dispersed he asked, "Lunching with the head of the company?"

"He's away today," she answered. "So—the usual place?"

He nodded eagerly and she was flattered. She had to be

honest with herself—she was not only flattered. Her pride, badly needing a boost after Jasper's dismissal, was purring quietly like a cat being stroked.

It was over the meal in the café that she began to wonder just why Leonard had sought her company and whether she had been too hasty in assuming that his eagerness to eat with her stemmed from his growing admiration for her as a woman.

"I'm going to see him, Alicia," Leonard said suddenly and with a touch of defiance.

The statement, Alicia thought, justified her private questioning of his motives in seeking her out.

"See who, Leonard?" she asked mildly, guessing the answer.

"Mr. Alexander. I'm determined to get myself out of the rut he's put me into. I want to do something meaningful in the way of design. I want to make my mark on industry. I know I've got it in me."

Alicia frowned, staring through the café window near which they were sitting. Mr. Seagar, tending to plumpness, his hair thinning, was passing. His suit was speckled with crumbs from the sandwiches he must have eaten on a park bench. Alicia was trying to work out Leonard's analysis of his own abilities. It was difficult sorting out the truth of his assertion about Todd Alexander, from his own perpetual chip-on-the-shoulder attitude to life.

"Mr. Alexander's out a lot," she said at last. "Mr. Seagar's in more often. And, judging by my own experience of him—" she kept her eyes away from Leonard's to ward off another comment about her relationship with Todd "—Mr. Seagar's more sympathetic and understanding."

"So the boss's shoulder, when you cried on it, was as

hard and unyielding as his character.'' Well, she hadn't averted the comment, but she didn't have to answer it. ''It's going to be the boss or nothing, Alicia. And if I don't get the design work I'm after—'' He left the sentence to finish itself.

Leonard's uncompromising attitude surprised her. Was he not the rather self-effacing individual she had always considered him to be? Sometimes she sensed that, beneath his reserve of manner, there was a dogged obstinacy, the kind that seemingly deferential people often possessed.

With a shrug she pushed away her cup. There was plenty of design work available that she was not allowed to divulge and there was no doubt that Todd Alexander would not disclose it, either. ''I wish you luck in trying to pin our employer down,'' she said.

To her knowledge, only one person had ever succeeded in doing just that—his ex-fiancée—and she had thrown him aside for another man.

Secretly, she felt sorry for anyone who thought they had ''caught'' Todd Alexander. There was a suspicion inside her that he might allow them to believe they had. He would no doubt play along with them for a while, then throw them back in the sea from which he had caught them—which meant that it was he, all along, who had done the ''catching.'' And—the thought came to her suddenly—the breaking up of his engagement.

As they left the café, she asked herself with alarm, *so why am I suddenly feeling sorry for myself?*

TODD HAD NOT RETURNED by the end of the afternoon. Alicia had been kept busy by Mr. Seagar who still preferred, he said, to have a nice-looking young woman to dictate to rather than an uninteresting machine. He had alternated his dictation with a few minutes' chat about life and people in general.

"You know where Todd keeps disappearing to, don't you?" he asked. Alicia shook her head. "To his beloved research project deep in the county of Hertfordshire."

Alicia murmured, "Oh, I see," then smiled to herself at Mr. Seagar's assumption that she was on first name terms with the boss. The mere thought stirred feelings inside her that rang warning bells.

"It's taken the place of a woman in his life," Mr. Seagar was saying.

"Was he—" Should she ask such a personal question about her employer? "Was he badly hurt when he discovered that his fiancée was playing around with another man?"

To her surprise, Mr. Seagar laughed. "Todd, hurt by a woman? I doubt if he ever took the engagement seriously. Did he tell you he was hurt?"

So I was right, Alicia congratulated herself, *in my supposition about Todd Alexander's attitude to women.* He manipulated their emotions until they thought they had enticed him into a relationship instead of the opposite.

"No, not hurt," she answered Mr. Seagar's question. 'I just assumed he was because of the bitter way he spoke about his ex-fiancée and about women in general. You know, their faithlessness."

"That empty picture frame?" So Mr. Seagar knew about that, too. "A reminder of women's vacillating nature, of their perfidy, and so on? He tells 'em all that, Miss Granger. That picture frame is really a Keep Off sign to the female sex in general."

"He said—he said he'd accept everthing a woman gave him as long as there were no strings."

"No marriage. Yes, I've heard it all. He likes his freedom to choose, use and discard. Well, it's true. He's just taking his time, that's all." He gave her a beaming smile. "I was well into my thirties before I committed myself to one woman, and it paid off. That was twenty years ago, and I still think I'm the happiest married man alive!" The smile this time was for himself, his much loved wife, his success in choosing the right marriage partner.

For a while he continued dictation, then leaned back in his chair. "What about you? I saw you at lunchtime eating with that young man, Leonard. Is there anything between you?"

From Todd she would have resented the direct question, but coming from this man, she took no umbrage at all. "We're just friends. I—" She looked down at her shorthand pad. "I've just been . . . discarded by my boyfriend. It still hurts."

"It will for a while, my dear, but believe me, it won't last. Someone else will come along."

Vehemently she shook her head.

"That young man, Leonard Richardson?"

"No, certainly not Leonard. *He's* not my type, but—" Her eyes lifted anxiously. He hadn't guessed, had he? His look was steady, but did it hold something else? And was it pity?

The dictation came to an end. Alicia went away to type the letters. Todd's office was not large, but in Alicia's imagination, without his presence it assumed all the characteristics of an empty echoing hall.

That evening she sat at home, watching television without

actually seeing what she saw. There was no losing herself in it, not in the comedy, the tragedy and certainly not the romance. When her heart was broken, how could she believe herself to be part of a love scene or the happy-ever-after ending?

"IS HE THERE?" Leonard was at the entrance to the general office next morning as Alicia approached it to use the photocopier. It stood near the door and at one end of the long room.

Pushing past him she answered, "He's not in yet."

For a few minutes he watched as she operated the photocopier although it was clear his mind was elsewhere. He said at last, "Could you let me know somehow when he does come in?"

She smiled at the sheets of paper that fell into place in the boxlike slots. "You mean send up smoke signals?"

He did not appreciate the mild joke. "There's a telephone on his desk."

"I've got my own extension now."

"Then use that, can't you? If someone in here gets to the phone here before I do, just say, 'Tell Leonard he's back,' or something."

"I'd have to listen for him coming. I couldn't pick up the phone and give that message when he was in the room. He'd think it odd. He's got that kind of mind. Anyway, I'll do what I can, although I won't make any promises."

Alicia was concentrating on typing the remainder of the letters that Mr. Seagar had given her the day before, and it was a few minutes before she heard the drone of voices coming through from his office. As soon as she recognized Todd's she grabbed the phone, punched out the extension number of the general office and drummed her fingers. The moment the call was answered she bent over the phone, as if hiding her face also hid her voice.

"Tell Leonard," she said quickly, "that he's here. Yes, he'll know—"

"Good morning, Miss Granger."

The telephone receiver crashed down out of control. For three or four seconds Alicia stared at her employer. He was at his desk. In leaving Mr. Seagar's office and walking to his seat, he must have heard every word.

The bright smile was switched on. The brightness invaded her eyes, too. "Good morning to you, Mr. Alexander."

There's a lilt in your voice of the perfect secretary. Quite an achievment after only one day. The equable temper and the desire to please—to stand on your head if the boss demands it—it's all there and only twenty-four hours out of the typing pool, too. Isn't it amazing what a lift up the status ladder and an increase in salary will do to a girl?"

Forcing herself to ignore the cutting words she said, "Thank you very much for giving me the job, and the extra money, Mr. Alexander."

He nodded, saying curtly, "You can switch off the artificiality. This is work, not play."

Twin flames burned in her eyes, but after a moment's struggle she dowsed them.

"You've found work to do?" Todd asked. "I understand Halmar Seagar's been keeping you busy." He flicked through the pile of opened letters. "Any phone calls?"

"I was able to cope with about two-thirds of them—"

He looked up. "Good." He smiled. "Only twenty-four hours a private secretary—"

"Personal assistant, you said, Mr. Alexander."

"Call it what you like—and no flap or fuss. No hassle or self-doubt. You're a find, Miss Granger." There was sarcasm again in the faintly drooping eyelids, the flick of the male gaze over her pale blue long-sleeved dress—although how much of the outer covering he was noticing and how much of the shapeliness beneath it, Alicia did not know.

He sat down. "These letters—some you can answer yourself. These I'll—"

There was a tap at the door.

Todd showed irritation. "Come in," he called. When the door opened to reveal Leonard's hesitant figure, Todd's eyes narrowed, slewing around to Alicia. She cursed the color that reddened her cheeks. It wasn't as if she was guilty of anything, except telling an employee that the boss had arrived, and what kind of crime was that?

Todd did not tell her to go but she had already decided that she could not sit there and watch Leonard squirm under the lash of Todd's tongue when he made his request for more interesting work. Leonard stood awkwardly in the center of the large room, looking first at his employer, then at Alicia, who was acutely conscious of Todd's suspicious regard. Did he think that she was in collaboration with Leonard?

Seizing some work, she hurried to the door, saying, "Excuse me," over her shoulder. She made for her old desk in the general office. When she found her concentration wandering so much that she grew worried about the standard of her work if she continued, she left the office and started in the direction of Todd's office.

When would Leonard come out? Had he been reduced to the size of a pottery miniature of himself by Todd's ruthless treatment? Taking refuge in the small kitchen, which was empty now that coffee time had passed and the women helpers had gone, Alicia wandered around, peering out now and then to search the corridor.

The moment she saw Leonard emerge from Todd's office, she moved from the doorway. Leonard joined her in the kitchen wearing a pleased look that somehow troubled her.

"He says he'll think about it," Leonard said.

"About different work?"

Leonard nodded. "He was really nasty, but I took it all, because you see I had a hold." His eyes shone blindingly like undipped headlights on a dark country road. Alicia found herself squeezing her own eyes shut until the unpleasant moment had passed.

Todd was 'nasty'? Leonard had 'a hold'! Her heart bumped like a car driving over a pothole. How could Leonard have 'a hold'? She had told him nothing. . . .

"You haven't implicated me in your machinations to get promotion?"

"I . . . er—" Leonard inspected his nails "—mentioned a certain . . . er . . . report, *secret* report, that you were typing."

Alicia felt ill, needing support, and leaned back against the stainless-steel draining board, feeling its coldness cut across her spine. "So you did implicate me!"

Leonard lifted his shoulders. "I knew about the report because I overheard Mr. Seagar whispering to you about it. The whispering made me suspect it was secret and you confirmed it by telling me that what you had to type was confidential. Then you took yourself off to some hiding place to work on it. You can't blame me if I piece together bits of information and use them to get something I want. After all, I'm ambitious. Not only that, I know that in there—'' he tapped his head ''—there's a lot of unutilized ability.''

"You think a lot of yourself, don't you?" Alicia commented. It was intended to be scornful but Leonard took it as an enlightened comment on his character.

"The world judges you on how you judge yourself. Or so they say, and I happen to think it's true. Anyway, in this kind of world, everyone's using everyone else all the time."

Alicia could not dispute that fact, but she could not forgive Leonard for linking her name with his. How much would Todd Alexander trust her now? And Mr. Seagar— would he curse the moment he decided that his faith in her integrity was such that he gave her that report to type?

"I didn't give any details of that report."

"I know, but I'm no fool. In a way I was groping in the dark. I put together two indisputable facts. I said you'd told me you were handling confidential material. I also said I was after a better design job. He drew his own conclusions and decided I knew all about everything via you."

"You tricked him!" Alicia accused, hands to her face. "Using in quite the wrong context, an innocent statement made by me to keep your greedy hands off the report. What you've done is something you can really feel proud of, isn't it? It would look good on your personal file if I told Mr. Alexander the truth, don't you think?"

His shoulders hunched, his head seemed to recede into them. "Stop threatening me, Alicia."

"Threaten? You think that was a *threat*? I want to keep my job here—and my boss's trust. I'm going this minute to put the record straight. I'm going to clear my name with Mr. Alexander."

"No use," Leonard called after her. "I've implicated you up to the neck."

She swung around and said violently, "Why, you—" She could not find words bad enough to finish the sentence.

Alicia knocked and entered, closing the door behind her.

Todd looked up coldly. "So you did get my message." She frowned and he explained, "I sent for you. I told Richardson to tell you. You were such a long time coming I wondered if your feet had turned so cold you'd grabbed your coat and got out fast."

"You're implying I'm a criminal. I'm not, despite anything Leonard might have said. And even if I were guilty, which I'm not, I'm no coward. I'd face the music, however raucous it might sound."

He stood and came around the desk, eyeing her up and down. "Don't try to be clever, talking in metaphors. It'll take all your wits to talk yourself out of this situation."

"Look, Mr. Alexander." She went up to him, eyes blazing. "First of all, I didn't get any message. I came here of my own free will. And second, I gave Leonard Richardson no secret information, none at all! Anyway," she said suspiciously, "just how much did he tell *you*?"

"Enough." His arms folded across his chest that, she knew by experience, was as hard as his character. "Enough to let me know I can't trust you any more than I can trust any other woman. But then I was never taken in by you, with your different roles—bubbling over like champagne, with your plastic-coated smile. Or conversely—" sarcasm tautened his mouth "—quiet and inviting as a polar ice cap."

"No, Mr. Alexander," she smiled coolly up at him, "it's you who's the refrigerated one, remember, not me. I told you that in your hotel bedroom."

His eyes narrowed, zooming in on her lips. She just prevented herself from stepping back. He wouldn't, would he? Not here at work. In the privacy of his bedroom—well, that was different, but here. . . .

"I don't know what you're thinking," his voice gritted, drawing color to her cheeks, "but I'm thinking of more mundane things—like firing you from your job."

CHAPTER FOUR

HE SMILED MALEVOLENTLY at her white shock.

"I've done nothing to merit being fired." Her answer was a quavering mixture of defiance and uncertainty.

"No? Betrayed my trust, not to mention Mr. Seagar's. Wouldn't that constitute sufficient grounds for dispensing with your services?"

Her self-assurance was seeping back. "Yes, if I'd done just that. Which I haven't."

"Leonard Richardson told me you told him about the new design job he might coerce from the boss, provided he used the right tactics."

"I did not tell him that! He overheard Mr. Seagar telling me about the report he wanted typed. That's all it was."

"Was it? He picked up the phone. "Halmar? Can you spare a few minutes?"

He came in at once. "Miss Granger." The man's faintly wrinkled face lighted up with his happy smile.

Todd's lips tightened at his colleague's easy, trusting manner, "This girl's been talking."

"I have not!" Her voice had risen and Todd's eyebrows lifted at her tone, but she did not care. She turned to Mr. Seagar for the support she knew she would get. "Leonard's been saying he knows about the secret report. He says that I told him about it. But what really happened, Mr. Seagar, was that he overheard you telling me about the reports."

Halmar Seagar shook his head. Alicia was aghast at his failure to come to her assistance. "Impossible for him to have heard. I whispered to you about them."

Her smile was weak yet pleading. "It was a stage whisper, Mr. Seagar."

The man smiled, looking at her in his kindly way. He could not, with his compassionate nature, have missed the dismay that dragged her shoulders down, pulled at the corners of her mouth. He glanced at Todd, whose eyes were hard.

"Well, yes, now. . . ." He rubbed his chin, which protruded from the pouched double one. "I seem to remember. . . ." Was he coming to her rescue, Alicia wondered, holding her breath. "Perhaps I did whisper loudly. My wife tells me I never can keep my voice down." Which was patently untrue, Alicia thought, flashing him a grateful smile, since his speaking voice was soft and warm.

Todd's smile was reluctant. "You wouldn't be playing the knight in shining armor, Halmar?"

Mr. Seagar gave two short laughs. His words, however, revealed the keenness of his mind. "Let's say I'm backing my hunch, Todd, my hunch about this very attractive young lady here. That she's the one person out of the whole staff I felt I could trust with that precious secret of ours."

Alicia's eyes grew moist and she could only smile her thanks as Mr. Seagar went from the room.

"Am . . . am I reinstated, Mr. Alexander?" she asked hesitantly.

"Are you trying to soften my heart as you've obviously softened Halmar's?"

She shook her head. "It would take a raging inferno to

do that.'' The smile that lurked about her lips was faintly impish.

Todd approached slowly, considering her mouth. "Is there a raging inferno inside you, Miss Granger?" His hands rested on her shoulders and moved to her throat. Her pulses leaped to frightening life under his touch. Somehow she had to repulse him. "That's something I'll never know,'' she replied, lifing her face boldly to his. "Now Jasper's gone I'll never let any man near enough to warm his hands.''

He pushed her away and she stepped back quickly to retain her balance. He resumed his seat while Alicia went to hers.

"Mr. Alexander?''

"Yes?" he answered curtly, across the large room.

"Did you let Leonard into the secret? Tell him about your other company?''.

There was no reply. "He implied that you had,'' she persisted.

Todd's eyes were on his work. "Now what do you think, Miss Granger?'' This time she could find no answer, but Todd did not go on.

After a few seconds, she said, "You mean you didn't?''

"I did not.''

So Leonard had tricked her into thinking he had tricked Todd Alexander into revealing the secret! Leonard was playing a very strange game.

"But Leonard led me to believe you had.''

"Did he indeed?'' If you want to know, I intend giving him a new job—designing components for the prototype of a vehicle that I'll tell him on the grapevine that one of the well-known car manufacturers is working on for future production. I shall motivate him by confiding to him that we're trying to beat the other company to it. His work won't be wasted and it will keep him happy. I'll also raise his salary by just enough to pare a layer or two off that chip on his shoulder.''

''So.'' Her sigh of relief was purely involuntary. ''I'm in the clear.''

''Did I say so?''

The question silenced her for a moment, then she asked again, ''Mr. Alexander, am I reinstated?''

''Miss Granger, you were never dismissed.''

ALICIA WAITED for the elevator on Friday morning feeling that the end of the working week could not come soon enough. So many things had happened she was unusually enervated.

There had been Jasper's letter that knocked her off balance from the start. Then had come her closer acquaintance with her employer, if that was how her intensifying relationship with him could be described. She was glad the elevator was empty as she stepped in. It meant that there was no one with whom she would have to make conversation.

So many events, she mused, had taken place in such quick succession, she had never really regained her balance. None of them, however, had erased her sense of desolation on reading that letter. Nor had they restored the self-confidence Jasper had so casually shattered.

Opening the door to Todd's office, she braced herself to face his hard, handsome face—only to find his chair empty. What made her gasp was the sight of the partition that had been put up to divide her section of the large office from the area that was Todd's.

So where was the entrance? She dived into the corridor. There, in the partition, was a door. It was obviously through that door that she was supposed to walk, shutting it behind her, out of sight and hearing of her employer—and his secrets.

Entering, she noted that together with the filing cabinets, her telephone extension had been moved in. Behind the door there was a cupboard for coats and personal belongings. A shelving unit had been added. In the center was an extra desk, smaller than her own. So she now had a fully-furnished office to herself.

Returning to Todd's office to retrieve her bag that she had flung down, she saw Todd entering behind her. Her eyes accused as she swung to face him. He reurned her gaze coldly and took his seat at his desk. He delved into his briefcase, ignoring the storm signals that emanated from her fiery eyes.

Spreading papers over the desk, he asked, "Haven't you any work to do?"

"Why has that been put there?" she demanded. He looked up blandly. "I thought I was going to be your personal assistant? That's what you called my new job."

"I changed my mind." He took a pen from his top pocket and began making notes.

"Because you don't trust me anymore?" His attention remained on the papers in front of him. "What am I supposed to do now—become the perfect secretary, behind bars?"

"Yes, Miss Granger. In your present mood, that would be a good place to put you. You—" he leaned back, looking her over "—have a shrewish streak. No wonder your boyfriend ditched you."

"Your girl friend ditched *you*, didn't she?" she hit back.

"Did she?" His voice was so mild it was a rebuke in itself.

Head high, she left his office and walked into her own, slamming the door. Then she stared through the patterned glass of which the upper part of the partition was made. Through it she could see the blurred figure of her employer. Remorse overcame her and she went out into the corridor and back into his office. "I'm sorry," she said.

At first, she thought he intended to ignore her. Then he replied, "Apology accepted," and continued writing as if nothing had happened.

Later he entered the small office that was now hers. In his hand was a sheaf of letters. "Answers scribbled on them. Put them into good English and leave them on my desk for me to sign. If I don't return in time, ask Mr. Seagar to sign in my absence. Right?"

With her eyes on the letters that were now on her desk she answered, "Yes, Mr. Alexander."

There was a silence. "Miss Granger," he said at last.

Her head turned and lifted. Her large, blue, weary eyes found his. He returned her gaze. "Are you still seeing Jasper when you look at me?"

She shook her head. "Only you."

He turned and went away.

AT LUNCHTIME Alicia entered the general office to find Leonard. It had become an established habit to have her midday meal with him.

He was so absorbed in the work he was doing he jumped when she stood beside his desk. "Alicia." His voice and high color reflected his inner satisfaction. "He called me in yesterday evening. Everyone had gone home. I've got everything I wanted out of him. I told you I'd got a hold—"

"Only by a clever bit of piecing together of events. Not to mention trickery," Alicia added.

For a moment Leonard looked pained. "Well, all's fair, et cetera, isn't it." He pulled a sheet of paper from below other papers. It bore a diagram and Alicia knew at once that it was the so-called prototype vehicle to which Todd had referred, saying he intended telling Leonard to design certain components for it. It bore a vague resemblance to diagrams she had seen attached to the reports she had typed.

Had Todd trusted Leonard, too, to keep the secret of the subsidiary company? Then she remembered he had said he would tell Leonard there was a rumor that a car manufacturer was also working on the design.

"What an odd shape," she commented, smiling. "Like an elongated grapefruit sliced in two and upside down."

"Ah," said Leonard, "that brings us to aerodynamics, and that's way beyond your comprehension."

Alicia could only agree with him there. "Does all this mean promotion?"

"More money, too, plus more interesting job."

"And all achieved by making Mr. Alexander believe I told you . . . certain things." She had so nearly given the secret away! She really would have to watch herself.

"You told me the reports were confidential. That was enough to set me thinking. So—" looking up at her "—now I know just what it was that was confidential."

Do you? she asked silently, but aloud she asked, "Are we lunching at the usual place?"

"Why not? I'll treat you to the meal. After all, you've helped me a lot, haven't you?"

Leonard in a happy mood was a pleasant enough companion. The meal was all the more enjoyable since Alicia allowed herself to choose one of the more expensive items on the menu. "You don't object?" she asked Leonard. "You're paying."

"Go ahead. I owe you something for the help you've given me."

Alicia frowned, not liking the way Leonard kept implying there was an involvement on her part in his successful attempt to improve his status. "You owe me nothing, really, Leonard. It was your own mind working overtime, putting one and one together and making three that achieved your object."

He shook his head in positive denial. "We're in this together."

"In what together?" Just how much did Leonard know, she wondered anxiously. Was it yet another trick on his part, making leading statements and hoping they would elicit information that would be of use to him in the future? "This—" he made a sweeping movement with his hand "—this confidential thing."

She clamped her lips shut, putting down the menu. If she said any more on the subject, she might find herself blurting out the vital information. Even an unguarded word could send Leonard's slightly devious mind hurtling off in all kinds of speculative directions.

They walked back to the office, passing Mr. Seagar leaving the building for his own lunch break. He smiled at them both and patted a bulging pocket. "I have my sandwiches. I shall sit on a bench in the park and eat them."

Alicia laughed as he went on his way. She called after him, "You seem to enjoy the simple life, Mr. Seagar."

"There's nothing like it," he called back, "for achieving peace of mind, even in the heart of overcrowded London!" He lifted a hand and was lost in the crowds.

Once again Todd had not returned by the end of the afternoon. A strange feeling of loneliness crept over Alicia as she sat at her desk listening to the silence from the office next door. Peace of mind, Mr. Seagar had said—it was a sensation that seemed to have eluded her that week. Without Jasper's phone calls, Jasper's company and Jasper's letters when he was away, the evenings seemed to have dragged.

Her eyes strayed to the patterned glass of the partition, seeking for a head-and-shoulders outline that wasn't there. Todd was away so much, she sighed. It had been unfair of him to remove her from the company of her colleagues and into his office, then cut her off from his presence.

Todd was nothing to her, she told herself firmly. So why did she miss him? In a very different way from Jasper, of course. Or was it? Was it Jasper's company she missed and not, as she had thought, his love? And was it Todd's company she missed, or Todd's—but there was no feeling between herself and Todd Alexander, let alone love. He had kissed her, comforted her, held her in his arms, but none of those things amounted to anything more on his part than passing diversions.

A deep sigh brought an end to the entanglement of her thoughts. The pile of letters awaiting Todd's signature would have to be taken to Mr. Seagar, as Todd had instructed. A tap at the communicating door leading to Mr. Seagar's office produced a cheerful invitation to Miss Granger to enter.

As Mr. Seagar added his signature to each letter, he said, "You're getting . . . very friendly with Leonard Richardson?'' Her hesitation had him adding, "Don't answer if you'd rather not.''

"I don't mind,'' she assured him. "We're little more than acquaintances, really. We lunch together quite often. He's rather a retiring person.''

Mr. Seagar seemed surprised. "You'd call him retiring?''

"Well, yes and no. On the surface, perhaps, but under it, I've got the feeling that when there's something he wants, he's . . . well, dogged and single-minded.''

"Mmm. A wise young woman as well as pretty to look at.'' He glanced up with a smile.

Alicia smiled her gratitude but as she returned to her own office, she thought, wise? Pretty? Even with her "stunning figure,'' as Jasper had called it, none of those things had had the power to prevent him from dropping her.

The telephone on her desk rang as she put the last letter into its envelope. Reaching out, she found her heart had begun to race up an imaginary stepladder. Todd, she wondered, speaking her name. It was Leonard and her heart went swooping down like a child on a playground slide.

"Guess what?'' Leonard asked. "I'm to have an office to myself.''

Alicia frowned. "On whose orders? Mr. Alexander's? But he's been out all day.''

"Mr. Seagar's just called me on the general office extension.''

"I've got some letters for franking,'' Alicia said. "I'm coming along now.'' Locking her desk and hoping that the girl responsible for dispatching the mail had not gone home, Alicia wondered at the curious step Todd had taken in giving Leonard his own office. She gathered the letters into a folder.

Checking on her appearance in the wall mirror, she decided it would pass. There would be no one meeting her on the way home, no one to impress. No Jasper, she thought, to inspect her—and silently criticize, as he must have been doing for some time before he walked off into another girl's arms.

Relieved to find the girl in charge still there, Alicia gave her the letters. Then she walked along the office to a beaming Leonard. "I'm a step nearer to becoming an executive," he boasted.

"That's a bit of optimistic thinking."

"No," he corrected her, "it's called positive thinking, something you've got to have in today's world."

Alicia frowned again. "I can't recall a spare office on this floor."

"They're going to create one by taking away an area from this office and putting up a partition, like they did for you. After all—" Alicia could almost see Leonard's pride inflating like a tire that had gone flat. "The work I've been given could be regarded as 'classified.' You know, confidential." The last word seemed to please him.

Alicia hoped wryly that, at some future date, his pride wouldn't develop a puncture. "Congratulations," she said. There was a dryness in her tone but she knew Leonard would not detect it.

She turned to go but Leonard retained her by saying, "Er . . . tomorrow. It's Saturday. Are you busy at all?"

"You mean will I be going out with my boyfriend?" Leonard nodded. "No, I haven't got a boyfriend now. I did tell you."

Leonard nodded again, remembering. "Can we go out

somewhere, a walk, a bus ride, something like that?'' He added, "I'd call for you."

Alicia thought, *not Leonard for the weekend as well as Leonard all week. . . . But if not Leonard, who else?* Her own company, and she had that all the time.

"That—" she took a breath "—that would be nice. About two o'clock? You know my address?'' He nodded. "See you tomorrow, then."

As Alicia approached the apartment block where she lived, she saw with surprise that there were net curtains at the windows of the left-hand ground-floor apartment. Plainly it was no longer for sale. Peering in one of the windows and with only the front yard lights to provide illumination, Alicia saw that wall-to-wall carpeting had been laid. It was impossible to distinguish the colors.

There were not many pieces of furniture, but packing cases littered the one room—the equivalent of her parents' living room—that she was able to see. Later, she decided, climbing the stairs, she would creep down and investigate, provided no one was there to see.

The arrival of a new family in the building added just a small oasis of interest to the desertlike waste of the weekend that stretched before her. Of course, though it was of little consolation, there was always Leonard's visit tomorrow to think about, not that she would allow it to occupy more than two minutes of her spare time!

Looking in a drawer for a clean apron to wear while cooking her evening meal, she found Jasper's letter. It had worked its way toward the back. If only that was where she could push it in her mind. Even now, as she reread the words, she experienced a sense of outrage mixed with helplessness.

What if she wasn't "full of life," didn't "enjoy dancing" and "going out" like his new girl friend, Loreen? She had her own personality, hadn't she? Her efforts to alter it had been wasted, she told herself, recalling Todd's amusement and even annoyance at her artificial smile and affected vivacity. Throwing the letter down, she picked up a saucepan and started to prepare the food.

After her meal and a rest, Alicia cleaned through the apartment. Despite the coolness of the late spring evening, the exercise had made her T-shirt cling to her moist skin. A shower, she decided, would cool her down. Since there was a movie on television that she wanted to see, she dressed in her nightclothes and pulled on her mother's quilted housecoat.

Curling up on the couch, she watched the end of the previous program, then became absorbed in the movie that followed it. To her surprise, she realized that she was no longer seeing Jasper's face instead of that of the main actor. In fact, even Jasper's name was beginning to sound strange on the rare occasions that she thought about him.

Had that rather cruelly worded rejection been more a blow to her pride than to her heart? Even as the satisfying thought that this must indeed have been the case was being accepted by her damaged ego, another and much more serious possibility was occurring to her. It was that her employer, Todd Alexander, might be in the process of taking Jasper's place in her mind.

The idea was so startling her attention wandered momentarily and her head flopped back onto a cushion. The office, even with the partition that now separated them, seemed like an echoing cavern when Todd was away. Yet at the rare times he was there the whole pace of her body's mechanism seemed to be speeded up, her mental processes in top form, his mere presence giving her working life a pivot around which to swing.

Not only her working life—he had invaded her private thoughts. Wasn't she lying there, eyes closed, picturing his strong features, his magnetic pull as his eyes searched and scanned, bringing color to her cheeks? And wasn't she imagining his arms around her again, his lips on hers, his shoulder beneath her cheek a she had sought comfort?

When she awoke, the television screen was blank, the traffic noise outside had lessened considerably. Operating the remote-control switch, she turned off the television set. In her bones she felt that the night had entered the small hours. And with her sixth sense she knew that it was not the nighttime silence that had wakened her, nor the fact that she was not in her bed. It was a noise that had come from the apartment beneath her own.

Swinging her feet to the floor, she crept to the bedroom, slipped shoes onto her bare feet, pulled a jacket capelike around her shoulders and opened the door that led to a tiny entrance lobby. Easing the main door open, she listened again.

There was the sound of boxes being moved—those cartons she had seen through the window? Had a thief broken in and was he now in the process of stealing everything he could lay his hands on? She did not know the family who were soon to move in, but she could not just stand by and allow all those possessions so trustingly left there to be stolen one by one.

If necessary, she told herself while creeping down the stone stairs, she could dive back to her parents' apartment and call the police. The main entrance door of the ground-floor apartment was wide open. Moving very slowly, she edged into the lobby. Putting her head around the living-room door, her eyes sought for the intruder. When she saw who that intruder was, she gasped and her fingers pressed her cheek.

"If you were after a burglar and thought you'd catch him unawares," Todd Alexander growled with heavy sarcasm, "he'd have run a mile before you got here. You made so much noise, even if he'd been deaf he would have heard you."

Now she was in the room and tugging at the coat around her shoulders. "All right, so I was noisy. But at least I was doing a good deed—or thought I was. If I'd known it was you and not the nice family I'd imagined had bought this place, I wouldn't have taken a step down those stairs."

"Right," he said. "Now you know I'm the new owner and not the thief you thought I was—" he raked in the packing case and straightened, holding a pottery jug "—you can go back to bed."

"I wasn't in bed."

The jug crashed to the floor, bounced on the carpet, then came to rest, having broken into three pieces. Its owner was left holding the newspaper in which it had been lovingly wrapped and staring unbelievingly at the remains of the jug.

His outraged gaze lifted to Alicia.

"It wasn't my fault," she said plaintively.

"If you weren't in bed, then where the hell were you in that outfit?"

"Asleep on the couch. I was watching a movie and I drifted off."

"Then you can drift off again—from my apartment."

"Why are you so bad-tempered, Mr. Alexander?" she asked, suppressing a yawn.

"What the devil do you expect me to be," he rasped, "when I'm tired to my very core, when I've just broken a jug I liked, when I've spent days attending to all the legal formalities involved in purchasing property and—" he advanced, fists on hips, toward her "—when I find you on the doorstep wanting in like a perverse domestic pet that's just been put out for the night."

His hair, usually so tidy, fell over his forehead. His tie had been dragged off and lay on the floor. His jacket was draped over a packing case, and his shirt was smeared with dust. There were perspiration marks under his armpits, and a film of moisture on his upper lip. The masculinity in him reached out to the femininity in her and she swayed toward him, her own fatigue breaking down all the barriers that, at normal times, existed between them.

His hands came up and gripped the soft muscles in her upper arms. Her hands rested against his chest and she looked into his eyes, squeezing her own as though she were looking at the sun.

Like a drinker who had just overstepped her limits, she said, "You've got smudges all over your face, Mr. Alexander." Laughter bubbled up from her throat and her head went down so that her forehead pressed against his chest.

For a few moments he let her stay there, then he forced her a hand's span away. "What's so funny about that?"

"Only that you don't look like Mr. Alexander at all. You look just like . . . ." Laughter rippled through her again. "A human being."

He jerked her close with a grip that had tightened. The jacket fell from her shoulders. The feel of him full-length against her was intoxicating and when a hand released an arm and hard fingers tipped back her head, she started swaying again.

"Have you been drinking?" he asked curtly.

Her head shook slowly. "It's just that I'm so tired, Mr.—" Her body was pressing against his now. "Why am I calling you 'mister'? Can I call you Todd?"

"Why not—Alicia?" Whether her lips pouted of their own accord or whether he initiated the kiss she could not decide, but his mouth claimed hers, gently playful at first, then lightly parting her lips. Gaining the admittance he had sought, the kiss turned ferocious, making her gasp at his audacity yet yielding to his mastery of her mouth.

When he released her, her legs were weak, her mouth bruised. Large, reproachful eyes stared into his but his comment was cynical. "You've seen nothing yet, honey girl. Tonight I'm near exhaustion. When in my normal state of vigor, you'd be surprised what I can do with a woman."

Working her way out of his hold, she drew her mother's dressing gown more tightly around her. "Well, I won't be here to be surprised. Find a woman more willing than I am—"

"That would be difficult," he commented dryly. As she turned he caught her arm. "Still seeing Jasper in my face?"

"No, again. I told you that this morning. I've put Jasper out of my mind. In fact, it's surprised me just how easy it is to forget a man, even if you think you're in love with him."

"Spoken like a true woman," he returned cuttingly. "My beloved ex-fiancée demonstrated how easy it was to forget the man she was going to marry even while she was still engaged to him."

"Then she can't have really loved you just as I can't have really loved Jasper. When the real thing comes along, it hits you—or so I'm told—right there." She pointed to her forehead. "Not to mention here." She patted the area where she thought her heart would be.

An eyebrow rose slowly. "So you know all about it."

Her head nodded, then realizing her error, she said clearly, "No."

He laughed at her confusion and turned away to face the task of unpacking. Looking around, Alicia asked, "Have you got anywhere to sleep?"

"The floor. It's carpeted, so—" Slowly he turned back to her, with a broad smile. "Why, are you inviting me to share—"

"No!" Her bruised mouth throbbed as his eyes came to rest on it. He smiled again and turned away. "Todd?" The name was spoken softly. It still seemed presumptuous to use it. "Would you like me to make you a cup of coffee?"

"Now that," he said, lifting out a stereo amplifier and lowering it with loving care to the floor, "would be a truly good-neighborly act." He glanced over his shoulder without rising from his crouched position. "Sure you're not too tired?"

"I am really," was her smiling answer, "but like the perfect secretary, I'm willing to go to any lengths to satisfy my boss's every whim."

He started to rise, anticipation in his eyes. "That bed you were offering—"

Alicia picked up her jacket, then turned and fled.

"I WISH YOU WERE always like this." They sat drinking coffee, Todd on an upturned packing case, Alicia on the floor.

As it was now two hours into a new day, it did not seem wrong to speak to her employer in such a personal way. His sleeves were rolled up, revealing arm muscles that, more than once now, she had felt imprisoning her body. His slacks were coated with a fine dust, his hair pushed back with impatient fingers.

The amusement in his brown eyes, eyes that until now she had seen flinty and cold, carried a query that invited her to continue.

"I mean relaxed and easy to be with, to talk to. . . ." Her eyes slid around to gauge his reaction. "To laugh with." He said nothing, swilling the contents of his cup. "Without the cynicism you carry around with you like . . . like a shield." His smile came and went. "Was it . . . ." She hesitated, wondering if the ground on which she was mentally treading would give way under her feet. "Was it your finacée's unfaithfulness that soured you so much, Todd?" His shoulders lifted. "Did you love her so much?" He frowned at the softly spoken question.

"What is this," he asked, after draining his cup and holding it out for more, " 'Confessions of a Boss to his Secretary'?"

Alicia refilled his cup. "In other words, it's none of my business."

"Precisely." He drank a mouthful and saw her yawn. "I would go to bed if I were you. Thanks for the coffee." If he thought that gratitude would send her on her way, he was wrong.

Alicia found that she did not want to leave him. "I some

how don't think I'd sleep if . . . ." She watched him empty his second cup of coffee. "If I knew you were down here just stretched out on the carpet."

Putting down his cup, he went over to her. She grasped his outstretched hand, allowing him to pull her up to face him. "How am I to take your concern for my welfare? Was that statement an invitation or honest concern?"

Her weary eyes held his "Concern, Todd, nothing else. Sorry to disappoint you."

His smile was strange, a little twisted. "Tell me what you've got in mind. If it's sleeping in your parents' bed, the answer's no, but thanks."

"It wasn't that. In the living room there's a recliner chair When it's fully extended, you can just drift off and wake up refreshed. That's why my parents bought it—them, really, because there are two."

"One for me, one for you." He took her hand.

Alicia laughed. "A chair for you, my bed for me."

"I can't make you change your mind? Not even—" he eased her against him "—this?"

She went into his arms, and it was curiously like entering a harbor after struggling against a storm. It was not just fatigue that made her compliant and consenting. Nor was turning to another man on the rebound the force that drew from her a response that curled her arms around his neck and put the promise of fire into her welcoming mouth.

The warmth and insistent pressure of his limbs against hers created in her a response that the tiny part of her reason that remained functioning could only wonder at. In the exceptional circumstances, it did not seem out of place to be in this man's arms—this man who, until so recently, she had known only as her employer, this man who had vowed never again to trust another woman.

The kissing, having reached a height, lingered then dampened down with a reluctant lifting of the lips. He held her away and looked into her face. "Which 'you' is this?" he asked, a smile curving to his mouth. "The brooding one, or the bubbling creature I dined with the other day?"

She shook her head, sweeping her hair against the strong arm that supported her unresistant body. "Neither."

The smile became set, the brown eyes deepening strangely in color. "Why, is there another personality I haven't yet encountered? A secret, counterfeit 'you' that you keep under lock and key?"

The words, probing, suspicious, had not been meant as a joke. Straightjacketed by his arms, she could not show her displeasure at his mistrust by breaking away. So her eyes and lips took up the challenge, although even their effectiveness as a weapon was muted by the unnerving nearness of his face.

"Do you ever wonder," she charged, "why your ex-fiancée carried on a love relationship with another man while officially being your wife-to-be? If you haven't, then I can tell you. Because you're all reason and no emotion. Where there should be warmth and giving inside you, there's only ice and selfishness. Even—" She saw the warning flash in the brown eyes, but pressed on. "Even a snow-drift offers more shelter and comfort than your—your warped personality."

The lips that zoomed in and overlaid hers were meant to inflict pain, the hard, male body against which she was pressed was intended to crush the breath from her lungs. The gasp that was wrenched from her was purely invol-

untary, expressing fear and helplessness at the hint of bar-
barity just beneath the surface.

When these invading lips softened to the brink of tenderness, when the hands that had been gripping her flesh
grew caressing, and when the painful angles and tough-
muscled limbs molded to her feminine softness, the sense
of relief that overcame her coaxed out of her an all-envel-
oping sigh. Tired beyond words, she lay against him eyes
closed. It was almost as if she had scaled an impossible
mountain, and against all odds, achieved the summit.

They remained embraced for long moments, in spite of
the whisper inside her that told her she had no right to be
where she was, at that hour of the morning, dressed for
bed. It was where she had, it seemed, always wanted to
be—in the arms of the man who, until only a few days
before, had been just a shadowy figure in her working life,
paying her salary and calling the tune.

As fas as she was concerned—and the thought took her
entirely by surprise—he could call the tune for her to dance
to for the rest of her life.

CHAPTER FIVE

ALICIA AWOKE next morning with the feeling that there was something different about life. When she remembered what that difference was—that a strange and disturbing presence was occupying her parents' living room—she swung her legs over the side of the bed and pushed her feet into her slippers.

Putting on a blue cotton negligee to match her nightdress, she combed her tumbled hair and opened her door. Her aim was to make an early morning cup of tea and she crept across the living room toward the kitchen, doing her best not to awaken her guest.

There was no need to walk on tiptoe, after all. That guest was awake and smiling broadly, not at her, but at a piece of paper held in one hand. Clutching her negligee at her neck and waist, Alicia frowned. Todd's smile lifted to rest on her.

"What's so funny about my appearance?" she queried defensively.

"Nothing." He returned to scanning the sheet of paper. He read aloud, " 'She's full of life. She enjoys dancing, going out. Other things, too.' " He lowered the paper, still grinning. " 'Get my meaning?' "

"My letter, my letter from Jasper!" Alicia ran, dived and grabbed—only to find the letter lifted high out of her reach. Unbalanced by the evasive action of Todd's hand, she found herself sprawled over him as he lay stretched out in the recliner chair. "Give it to me!" she demanded. "It's private. It's meant for me alone."

Todd's free arm came to rest across her back as effective a trap as if a tree had fallen on her in a gale. He held the letter high. " 'Sorry about it, but—' " Todd continued reading "—'no hard feelings?' " He dropped the letter to the floor and looked down into Alicia's face. It was indignant and flushed and held stiffly away from him, just below his chin. "Well," he asked, "do you have those 'hard feelings'?"

"Did," she mumbled, "not do. Got over it now. Will you please," she spoke through her teeth, "let me go?"

He ignored the plea. "So it didn't go as deeply as all those tears that evening suggested? Seeing his face in mine." He shook his head with mock solemnity. "Are you always so fickle in your affections?"

"Look—" She wriggled irritably against him but at his curt order to keep still, she obeyed at once. The small knowledge she possessed of male reaction to a woman's movements forced her better judgment to prevail over indignation. "I only knew him for two months. Our . . . acquaintance flared up, roared like fire for—what . . . four, five weeks? It wasn't very long. Then it died down. I began to see his personality separately from his surface attractions."

"And he you?"

"Must have." Her eyelids squeezed shut. Todd's fingers were under her chin but she refused to look into his searching eyes. "He saw—"

"Let me guess," he interrupted dryly. "The girl who likes the quiet things in life, who didn't want the loving without the love. Tell me—'' his fingers on her chin tightened ''—how often did he ask for . . . the 'other thing'?''

Her chin jerked free. ''That's my business.''

''But you wouldn't give?''

''That's also my business.'' Her teeth were clenched. When his hand fitted around her throat forcing up her head, she kept her eyes wide open this time. He would see no sign of her newly discovered love for him. That had been slipped into a hiding place in her heart. All he would see was defiance, plus a growing discomfort arising from her strained position across him.

It seemed, however, that he also saw something else, something that answered an unasked question. The smile that flicked across the sensual mouth indicated an inner satisfaction. ''No, you wouldn't,'' was all he said.

''Will you let me go? I was going to ask,'' she added, ''if you'd like a cup of tea.''

''Only if,'' the brown eyes narrowed as if in anticipation, ''it's sweetened with a taste of honey. In advance.'' His mouth warmed hers to startled life. ''The man,'' he murmured lazily, lifting his head and watching as she struggled off him and straightened her nightclothes, ''must have been crazy. Or blind.'' He eyed the flush his kiss had created. ''Or both.''

ALL MORNING there was the noise of coming and going from the apartment below. Great lumbering delivery vans turned into the front parking lot of the apartment block. Men who did not look strong enough to hold up an umbrella, carried in tables, dining chairs, armchairs and kitchen equipment.

Todd had left after drinking the tea Alicia had made. He

had refused her offer of a clean towel and the use of the shower. He had brought a suitcase of necessities, he told her, but thanks all the same.

"Thank you, also—" his smile had been mocking "—for the night's free accommodation, and for the hidden extras, also free."

Alicia's anger was instant and his laughter filled the room. "Don't lie with your eyes," he remarked. "You enjoyed the kissing as much as I did."

Her glare melted into a responding smile. "Maybe I did. On the other hand—" She half turned back. "Maybe I didn't."

"Baiting me back into your pool, Miss Granger? If I swallowed the bait, I warn you, you'd follow it, tumbled hair, pouting lips, big serious eyes, and all."

Then he had gone and she had been left alone, missing his dynamism immediately.

Halfway through the morning she followed two men maneuvering a large refrigerator into the kitchen. "Coffee, Todd?" she asked, interrupting as he gave precise instructions to the men about the placing of the piece of equipment.

"Thanks," he answered shortly. They might have been back at the office. Resentment flared at the man's retreat behind his familiar glacial manner.

"Three?" she asked. The other men's response contained the gratitude missing from that of the apartment's new owner.

Carrying down the tray of coffee, she distributed the mugs, saying, "If there's anything I can do—"

"Just keep out of the way," Todd answered, accepting the coffee she handed him.

"That's the way to talk to the wife," one of the men

said, raising his coffee mug to Alicia as if proposing a toast. His companion laughed in agreement, sipping a mouthful and commenting that he wished *his* wife made coffee like this.

Alicia looked quickly at Todd, expecting to see annoyance. Instead, he lifted his mug, too. "To my wife," he mocked, his lids slightly lowered, "and may she always do as she's told."

The other men grinned broadly. When Alicia said, with a honey-sweet smile, "Next time you want coffee, love of my life, go out and buy it!" they added their loud laughter to Todd's.

The telephone in the living room rang as Alicia prepared her midday meal. Answering the call with a pleasantly inquiring, "Granger residence," she almost jumped when a familiar voice said, "Want to come down and see the finished product?"

"Your instructions to me," she flipped back, "were to keep out of the way. So the answer's 'no.' "

"I'm inviting you to my apartment warming."

"What, right now?"

"Right now. You and me. A cozy twosome. You wouldn't refuse to drink to my future happiness in my new home, would you? Consider the implications. Get on social terms with the boss and who knows where it might lead in this world of business we both move in."

"You're joking, Mr. Alexander. I never, ever, crawl." There was a thinking pause. "I'll come down and pick up my parents' crockery."

As soon as she stepped into Todd's living room, her hand was taken and her fingers wrapped around a glass. Her face was flushed from her labors over the preparation of her lunch and his relaxed coolness irked her. He wore a round necked, dark brown, cable-stitched sweater over his open-necked shirt. His slacks were brown, his dark hair soft and freshly brushed.

·The ridged cheekbones tapered to the square, determined chin. All this she usually saw in conjunction with an un-smiling mouth and emotionless, businesslike eyes. At that moment, however, the eyes gazed as warmly as the mouth was smiling. Was there also a veiled "got you where I want you" mockery lurking behind the surface good humor?

"Your move," he prompted. "I can't drink to myself and my own health and future happiness in my new home."

"I thought ," she responded tartly, "that there was noth-ing Todd Alexander couldn't do?" She ignored the nar-rowing eyes. "That's the impression his underlings are given when he honors the office building with his pres-ence."

The lowered eyelids lifted, revealing a sarcastic amuse-ment. "I'll be modest and admit there's little. I could, for instance . . . ." The brown eyes turned faintly malicious. "With very little effort—" his eyes swept the shape of her "—make you the first woman to share my newly made-up bed in there." He nodded toward a door that Alicia knew from her parents' apartment led to a bedroom.

"You think so?" As a challenge it was a brave but abor-tive effort.

"I know so."

Had Todd guessed her secret—that she loved him? She colored faintly then covered her embarrassment by lifting her glass with a dazzling smile and saying, "To the health and future happiness of Mr. Todd Alexander in his new home. And may the ice in his nature melt in its centrally heated warmth.''

''Why, you little—''

Alicia took a step back and urged dramatically, ''Drink, drink, or the toast will burn to a cinder!''

''You know what you are?'' The narrowed look was back. ''An impudent—'' He broke off to taste and finish his drink at one gulp. His glass was placed with a thump on a low table. Alicia put her half-empty glass on the windowsill and turned for a getaway. He was there in the doorway.

His arms were lifting her and her hands were gripping his shoulders to hold him away. ''No, no.'' The words were pure reflex, a woman's first and traditional barrier. Her body reacted so differently, the strength of its will frightened her. *How could it be so*, she wondered frantically. *I'm not two separate people—mind and body. They're one entity, they form a whole. If my mind says, 'Relax,' just like it's doing, then my body relaxes.*

So it's my mind, she thought, dreamily watching those lips descend, *that's putting my arms around his neck, making my mouth cling to his, never wanting the moment to end. . . .*

As his head lifted, she saw the grooves from nose to mouth, the movement of the hard jaw as if his teeth were pressed together. She saw the satisfaction in his glance give way to gratification at the easy conquest. Below all this, she perceived the glinting frost that no woman, he had vowed, would ever melt again.

Closing her eyes, she withdrew into herself. The effort was enormous, for she knew for certain now that she was deeply in love with the man. Nothing could save her from the pain she knew would follow, but the least she could do was to hide her feelings from the man himself. Without asking for her release from his arms, her feet were lowered to the floor. Opening her eyes, she tried to discover whether his keen brain had decoded her body's messages. His gaze was as withdrawn as her manner now was. It was as if the embrace had taken place in her own imagination.

At once she turned around toward the room. It was, she decided, time to sail into safer waters. Hadn't she, after all, been invited to see the "finished product"?

"I admire your taste," she commented. "Those armchairs, that couch, the curtains—" she looked across the room "—the sideboard." She breathed in. "Mmm, leather, none of your man-made stuff. Velvet, real wood with the tang of the forest still on it. And just look at that grain." Her fingers rested on a wooden cart. "No veneer for Mr. Alexander."

"No veneer on my women, either." His lazy smile waited for the hit back. It never came.

Her legs carried her into the bedroom, where her praise began again. "Who did all this?" When I left you, the men were still delivering the stuff."

"The experts arrived soon after you'd gone. It was all arranged in advance. They hung the curtains, arranged the kitchen."

"Made the bed?"

"Disappointed? Were you counting on entertaining a guest in your apartment again tonight?"

The thought had crossed her mind but she kept her expression under control. Her gaze roamed—and checked. The picture frame—it was there, beside the bed. Looking straight at it, she saw once again the dulled reflection of her own face, bearing this time not surprise but a touch of despair.

As she turned away, she wondered if he had seen her expression. His next remark could be taken either way. "Yes, Alicia—" his lips speaking her name momentarily halted her breath "—it's on display, that reminder to me of woman's untrustworthiness."

That, she reflected, was a curious word to use. "When I first saw that empty frame," she recalled, "you said it was a woman's 'inconstancy and faithlessness' you wanted to be reminded of. Why are you now adding 'untrustworthiness' to the list?"

His half-smile and raised eyebrows gave Alicia the impression that he was waiting for her mind to provide the answer. Two or three seconds later, it was there in her head, but in the form of an incredulous question. "You're not implying that Mr. Seagar's trust in me about the secret research was wrong?"

"Since you've asked," he replied, "the answer's yes. But now the damage is done—"

"Damage?" she retorted furiously. "What damage?"

He went on, ignoring the interruption. "If you ever let me down," he moved nearer, menace in his eyes and stiffened arm muscles. "If you so much as breathe the slightest hint to any other person about Sander Design and its near-breakthrough I'll do this—" his fingers fitted around her neck, tightening until her heartbeats hurt "—until you cry out for mercy."

His brown eyes turned her blue ones cold. It was as if icicles were dripping into them until they overflowed. "Please," she gasped, "let me go. I promise again that I won't say a single word to *anyone*."

"Except those already involved." With difficulty Alicia nodded and as his fingers eased, she could not prevent the accumulated tears from dropping onto his hands. Something—had it been her promise or her tears—thawed his frostbitten mood. The hands around her neck became caressing and his mouth lowered slowly, slowly to still and hold her trembling lips.

When the kiss was over, its taste lingered, its tenderness leaving in its wake a weakness of her legs and a tingling down her spine. The masculine mouth that had created the havoc had softened into a curious smile, but its message was as indecipherable as mirror writing in a foreign language.

He had turned from ice to sunshine in the space of a few seconds. Where this tantalizing man was concerned, it was not only his top secret company that was kept hidden, it was his true character. Had even his ex-finaceé been allowed to know it? Smoothing her shoulder-length fair hair and flipping the curled ends through her fingers, she said, with a smile that still held traces of his mouth's magic touch, "I've been cooking my lunch. There's enough for two."

"The answer's yes, thanks. The aroma drifted down and tantalized my nostrils." An arm rested casually across her shoulders.

"So now I know," Alicia said, laughing as they mounted the outside stairs, "why you really invited me down."

"You have a keen mind, Miss Granger," he mocked. "How good are you at cooking?"

"You'll soon find out. It's nothing elaborate," she explained. "Steak and kidney pie."

"Lead me to it," he said.

After the meal, as he dried the dishes that Alicia had

washed, he asked, "Do you usually cook twice the amount of food you know you're going to need?"

She threw him an impish smile. "Only when a new neighbor's just moved in and he's tall, dark and—" she eyed him up and down, giving a dreamy sigh "—*very* handsome."

He handed her back the tea towel. "What's in your mind?" he drawled, eyeing her lazily. "A raise in salary? Or something more personal?" Her cheeks turned pink, which seemed to amuse him. "Come on," his voice was low and deep, "I think we know each other well enough now to be honest about such things."

Her words, she had to admit, had been provocative. Knowing the man, as he had just said, better now, she should have been more cautious. She should have anticipated the hard, expectant look that would spring into his eyes.

Self-defense was necessary—strictly verbal, of course— before the fuse of desire was ignited. Physically, she was well aware, glancing at his tough physique and recalling the strength of his arms, that she would be helpless in defending herself from him.

"You've chosen the wrong woman," she returned, more calmy than she felt. "I've been rejected by a man, just as you've been rejected by a—"

"I did the rejecting." His voice was curt. Only a scratch of the surface, she mused, was sufficient to reveal the solid ice that was this man's makeup.

"Sorry. I was going to say that I've forsworn men just as you've—"

"I haven't forsworn women. Only marriage."

"Sorry again." She untied her apron and folded it neatly.

"Anyway, I'm not angling for a raise and—" her eyes held his steadily "—nor do I want any kind of casual relationship."

"Your actions belie your words. Every time you've been in my arms, every time I've kissed you, your body has given me 'come on' signals."

She dropped her apron, picked it up and refolded it. The words he had spoken were facts and she could not dispute them. There was a sudden lump in her throat. Of all the men around that she could have fallen in love with, why did she have to choose this heartless member of the species?

"Sorry," she said yet again, and this time it was a whisper.

He was in front of her now, lifting her chin, searching her eyes like an expert examining precious jewels for flaws. "Don't be sorry. Shall we call those signals a perfectly natural reflex action on your body's part?" She nodded, lowering her eyes, but knowing he was now scanning her face.

They weren't conditioned reflex, her lips clamored to tell him, they arose from the wish to be loved back in the same way as she loved him. But her lips trembled instead.

In an instant his mouth had stilled the tremor. At his touch her passionate nature, which even Jasper had never come to know, broke free and her arms went around Todd's neck. His response was immediate and she was against him, his arms hard as steel around her. Her brain whispered, "Fool." Her heart told her otherwise.

"Alicia?" The voice came from the living-room door It was uncertain yet determined and it could belong only to one person. "The front door was slightly open, so I came in."

Take these 4 best-selling novels FREE

Take these 4 best-selling novels FREE

Your FREE gift includes

Sweet Revenge by **Anne Mather**
Devil in a Silver Room by **Violet Winspear**
Gates of Steel by **Anne Hampson**
No Quarter Asked by **Janet Dailey**

Take these **4** best-selling Harlequin romance stories **FREE**

exciting details inside

Todd's arms were gone from her at once. His eyes moved cynically from Alicia to Leonard, then back. "Next time you're expecting a visitor," he said to Alicia, "warn me, will you? Then I won't eat the food you've prepared for him. Nor will I kiss his girl."

With burning cheeks Alicia flung back, "Wrong again, Mr. Alexander, on both counts. Leonard never intended to come for lunch. And I'm not his girl!"

IT WAS NOT EASY descending from the heights to which Todd's presence had lifted her. It was even more difficult adjusting her mood to the level that Leonard's heavy-going personality required.

"Sorry if I came at an awkward moment," Leonard said, "but I didn't know there was anything between you and Mr. Alexander."

"There isn't," Alicia said grimly, "nothing at all. He was just getting a . . . a bit fresh with me." Which, she thought, was grossly unfair to Todd, but wasn't he being unfair to her treating her as if she were his woman? "He's bought the apartment downstairs," she explained. "He only moved in yesterday. He never even warned me what he'd done."

Leonard did not seem unduly worried about the situation and let the subject drop. When he suggested going for a walk, Alicia agreed with relief. The weather was bright without being overwarm, the shrubs in the suburban gardens were in full bud if not in bloom. It did at least give her something to do, she thought with amusement—trying to judge when the spring flowers would break into blossom.

Also, for a time, it acted as a subject of conversation. What had possessed her, she wondered, to agree to Leonard's suggestion that he might visit her? Then she remembered that it was before she knew the empty apartment below would become occupied, and, more important, before she knew the identity of the new occupant. If she had known, she would have kept Leonard away at all costs.

Back at the apartment, he sat on the couch and talked of his future in the firm, how bright it looked now he'd been given his own office. Alicia did not spoil his pleasure by pointing out that she, too, had been given an office to herself. When she went into the kitchen to make an afternoon cup of tea, Leonard continued to talk about himself. It was a subject that interested him to the exclusion of everything else. For a few moments he did stop and Alicia sighed with relief. The silence didn't last and when she carried in the tray, Leonard's voice was still droning on.

The tea was drunk, the conversation continued, veering away from Leonard's affairs, but not from the office in general. As the time approached for an evening meal, Alicia hoped fervently that Leonard would not stay so long she would have to invite him to share it with her.

An afternoon of him was all she could stand, she told herself desperately. As she started experiencing hunger pangs, she actually willed him to go. Maybe he got the message, she thought wryly, because he stood up at last and looked at his watch. "I must be off," he said.

And those, Alicia thought, *are the sweetest words I've heard in months!*

"I'm meeting a friend for a drink tonight," he added. "Someone I worked with in my last job, before I joined Alexander's."

When he had gone, and Alicia had climbed the stairs to her parents' apartment, a sense of loneliness descended

The empty silence of the ground-floor apartment told her that her new neighbor was not at home.

SUNDAY MORNING brought with it the usual feeling of luxury, of leisure time to be spent exactly as she wanted. So she pulled the covers over her shoulders and settled down to sleep again—until she remembered Todd. Instantly wakeful, she swung back the bedclothes and ran to the bathroom, surprised at how late it already was.

Emerging, she dressed in cord slacks and bright yellow blouse. A comb brought her hair to relative order and she dashed into the kitchen to make toast and coffee. Settling down at the breakfast bar with the morning paper, Alicia crunched her way through the toast. She had reached her second cup when the doorbell rang.

Todd was there, holding out a jug. His dark green shirt was rolled to the elbows, and the slacks he wore were creased in the wrong places. The belt around his waist drew attention to the lack of surplus flesh around his middle. The sight of the man on the doorstep turned a quiet Sunday morning into a clangor of amplified heartbeats and a rushing in her ears—which was, she reassured herself, only her own blood racing through her veins.

"Sorry to disturb you." His broad smile belied his words. "But—"

"You forgot to arrange for a milkman to call." Alicia shook her head in mock despair. "You need a woman in your life."

He stepped inside, giving her the jug. "Any offers to fill the vacancy? Or—" his eyelids twitched like a stage curtain before a performance "—are you already spoken for?"

"Yes," she answered promptly, "by a dream man who doesn't exist."

The smile returned. "So abandon your dream and accept the next best thing. A flesh and blood male, surname Alexander."

In the kitchen, Alicia filled Todd's jug. She smiled at the creamy white liquid. "Are you offering yourself to me, Mr. Alexander?"

"On a purely temporary basis, yes." She could hear that he, too, was smiling.

"Would my photograph go in that empty frame?" She flung an impudent smile his way.

He smiled faintly at her provocation but his voice was hard. "That frame stays empty until I find the woman I decide to take as my wife."

"Your dream woman, just like my dream man—nonexistent outside romantic books and films?"

"In that case," he lifted a dismissing shoulder, "it stays empty. Until the woman of my choice makes an appearance, other women will do very nicely, thanks."

"Count me out, Mr. Alexander." He took the filled jug from her. "I've always refused to be one of a number."

"I'll bear that in mind, Miss Granger," he mocked. At the door he lifted the jug. "Thanks for this. By the way, how did your afternoon and evening with the boyfriend go?"

"Afternoon," she corrected firmly. "And—it went, thanks."

"Are you trying to get me to believe he didn't stay until he and you—"

"He and me nothing!" she snapped. "I meant what I

said about nonentanglement after Jasper. Did you," she countered, overly sweetly, "enjoy your evening out?"

"Very much. Keeping a check on your new neighbor's movements, Miss Granger?"

Alicia colored and smoothed her flowered apron. "I saw your place was empty when I showed Leonard out just before I cooked my meal." Her eyes lifted defiantly. "Nothing wrong with that, was there?"

"Nothing at all," he responded with a smile that contradicted his guileless tone. He lifted the milk jug as if proposing a toast and disappeared through the doorway.

As she ate a solitary lunch, Alicia felt lonely. The idea of inviting Todd to share it had occurred to her, but she had dismissed it. She did not wish to appear to be encouraging a closer relationship between them—despite the fact that nothing would make her happier, hurt though she might be by his eventual dismissal of her from his life.

Wandering around the apartment for a restless hour, she opened the main door, then closed it again. Why shouldn't she go down those stairs, step outside and take a few breaths of air? If, on the way, she happened to meet Todd . . . .

Todd was nowhere to be seen, but his door stood invitingly open. As if her head and shoulders were a toy on a string, they were pushed into the small entrance hall, followed quickly by the remainder of her body. Some irresistible force was urging her forward into his living room.

It was no use her brain telling her, "This man is not just your neighbor, he's your boss, too, so you shouldn't be here without his permission." Her legs were deaf to the warning and took her into the kitchen. It was plain that a quick salad meal had been eaten, as the used dishes were stacked on the draining board.

It would give him a pleasant surprise, she thought, if these were clean when he came back. No sooner thought than done. . . . The dishes were washed, dried and stacked for putting away. That done, she wandered back to the living room. Curiosity as to whether he had bothered yet to furnish the second bedroom—the equivalent of hers—took her through its door.

She caught her breath. Around the walls were wooden tables, across the center a desk with doors that were wide open, revealing shelves and pullout trays. Standing on one of the tables was a drawing board. Rulers, pencils and piles of paper covered the table tops. There were sketches, ruled drawing and roughly executed automobile designs.

"Spying on my company's research project, Miss Granger?"

CHAPTER SIX

THE WORDS STUNG like a fistful of stones flung from the doorway. Her face was scarlet at Todd's interpretation of her presence in what appeared to be his private office. Deciding to counter his accusation with a joke, she answered, "Yes, I've got a miniature camera hidden in my slacks pocket."

To her astonishment, Todd approached, his gaze holding hers so fixedly she could not tear hers away. Standing in front of her, his unreadable expression never changing, he gripped her shoulders and jerked her against him. Then, while one hand held her still, the other slid down her side, over her breast and waist, until it found her hip. His fingers then proceeded to invade the side pocket, searching it thoroughly.

Alicia's breathing quickened and she said, "Will you stop it!" Far from sounding like the reprimand she had intended, it emerged as a breathy whisper. As if she had not spoken, he changed hands and sides and repeated the exercise, not only delving into the second slacks pocket but sliding his palm to her rear, where his searching fingers investigated the back pocket.

His smile was taut as he thrust her away.

"You didn't honestly believe," she said hoarsely, "that I had a camera hidden? You didn't really doubt my honesty so much you thought I'd—" her hand moved to indicate

the drawings and designs "—sink so low as to take part
in industrial espionage?"

His failure to reply infuriated her. She lifted her arms
wide. "Go on, do the job thoroughly," she stormed.
"Search me from top to bottom. Subject me to the indignity
of making me strip." Her tongue was taking as much notice
of her brain's warnings as her legs had earlier.

When his lips twisted from the thin line into a humorless
smile, she recognized the invitation that could be read into
her words.

"Alicia, the beautiful spy," he mocked. "Okay, un-
dress." An eyebrow quirked at her white face. "It was your
suggestion. If you don't, I'll do it for you." She was trans-
fixed by the thrusting jaw, the full, tormenting lips.

"Don't be silly." Her throat was so dry she could hardly
speak.

A step brought him closer. His hands, gripping the neck
of her blouse, jerked until the buttons came open. Her hands
went up to tear at his, nails digging into his knuckles. Then,
to her profound dismay, her muscles started to misbehave,
just as her legs had done.

Her palms softened, her fingers changed their mind,
pressing instead of pulling. As his hands sought and found
her feminine shape, his eyelids drooped, darkening the
brown of his eyes. "Todd," she whispered. "Oh, Todd."

His arms were around her, and her body grew pliant and
yielding. When his fingertips found the racing beat of her
heart, his mouth took hers and she was lost.

When the kiss was over, she grasped the material of his
shirt, fearing that her legs might give way. His hand stayed
where it was and their eyes locked.

"Are you," he asked softly, breaking the spell, "offering

yourself to me now, instead of the other way around?'' He was back to mocking and Alicia's heart sank. If only there was a vulnerable spot about him that she could discover and use to help her convince him that if he were to make her his, for life, nothing in the world would cause her to let him down as, it seemed, the woman who had embittered him had done.

''Please,'' she said and fastened her fingers around his wrist. There was a moment's hesitation before she pulled at it, a moment in which she wished with all her heart that she could, without loss of self-respect, give him the right to hold her so intimately. ''Please take your hand away.'' He did so at once.

When her blouse was rebuttoned, she asked, ''Todd, you didn't really think I'd do such a thing?''

His hands slipped into his slacks pockets. ''Act the tame spy?'' He considered her for a few seconds, put fingers to her chin, searched her face. ''You have big, honest, blue eyes,'' he mused. ''A mouth that's not only honey-sweet but from it's inviting shape could surely speak only the truth.'' There was still no positive answer.

''Do you trust Mr. Seagar?''

''Implicitly.''

''Well,'' triumphantly, ''*he* trusts me, otherwise he wouldn't have let me in on the secret.''

There was a long, agonizing pause. Was he struggling against his better judgment? He said at last, ''Let's give you the benefit of the doubt, shall we?''

Her smile was like sunshine from a cloudless sky. ''I washed your dishes.''

''In your role as perfect secretary, or perfect wife?''

''Both.'' She was impudent again, but surely they could

be friends, if not lovers. By his broad smile, he did not seem to mind.

"I'll remember that. I'm beginning to be glad I bought this place. With you as a neighbor, I won't be lacking for anything." He considered her mouth. "Will I?"

Her smile put a brilliance in her eyes. "Nothing," she agreed.

His head lowered, his hands gripped her arms. Any moment now she would be in his arms again and she panicked. "Todd, please, not now. . . ."

His mouth was homing in. "Relax, my love. It's the weekend. Classify it as a leisure-time activity." Her lips were immobilized and she could not reply. Her arms locked around his neck.

The telephone rang. The pressure against her mouth eased and he murmured, his lips feathering hers, "Damn the thing. Why didn't I take it off the hook?"

He grasped her wrist and led her to the bench on which the telephone stood, demanding immediate attention. With his right hand he pushed something aside then lifted the receiver.

"Alexander here. Roy? What? Have you interrupted my Sunday siesta?" He glanced around at Alicia then answered, smiling broadly, "Almost. No, it's of no consequence." At Alicia's indignant tug, he merely tightened his grip. As he talked, she realized he was discussing his secret project. Words such as "power units," "catalytic property" and "flexible system" registered vaguely in her brain, yet through lack of technical knowledge, made no impact at all.

All the same it struck her that she shouldn't be there, overhearing the exchange of highly confidential information. With a painful twist she was free and making for the door. She heard the clipped instruction to the caller to "Wait a moment," then he was gripping her shoulders and jerking her backward.

Forcing her to stand beside him, he captured both her wrists, pulled them behind her back and secured them in a merciless grip. With his other hand he picked up the receiver and resumed the conversation.

By the time it was over, she was exhausted by her abortive struggles and bruised by the useless twisting of her imprisoned wrists. Still holding her, he leaned sideways against the long wooden table. Her flushed cheeks and indignant eyes seemed to amuse him.

"That's given you something to think about," he commented. "I hope you absorbed every word and memorized every detail, because on my desk tomorrow I'll want a typed copy of the conversation."

"You must be joking."

He laughed, throwing back his head. "You look as if I've just committed you to a life sentence. And I'm not joking. I'll have that typed copy—or else." He made a slicing motion with his hand across her neck. "Or else it's the chop."

"But, Todd—" his finger idly smoothed away her deep frown "—you should have given me warning. I did my best *not* to listen. And anyway, you might have been speaking a foreign language. I'm not a scientist or engineeer or whatever. Just a simple little typist who does as she's told. And, Todd . . ." she put her head on one side. "Please let my hands go."

"Okay, but reluctantly. I like having you in my power." He twirled an imaginary mustache. "All the same, Alicia,

I meant what I said. Look.'' His arm went across her shoulders and he pulled her toward the table. "All the while I was speaking, I had a pocket cassette recorder working, picking up not only what I said, but Roy's conversation, too. Play the recording back tomorrow in your office, typing it as you go, maintaining strict secrecy, of course. I'll want twenty-five photocopies made. Okay?''

"I could—'' She turned on him. "I could *do* something to you, Mr. Alexander, scaring me like that!''

He laughed, pulling her around. "Do I scare you?''

Slowly she nodded, whispering, "You scare the living daylights out of me.''

He grew serious, his eyes darkened. "My sweet, I—'' The kiss was inevitable and this time Alicia responded unreservedly and with passion, giving kiss for kiss, telling him with her lips but not with words, just how much he had come to mean to her.

With his caressing hand lingering on the full swell of her breast, he looked deeply into her eyes. It might, in another man, have been a look of love. Even in this man, she wondered hastily, linking her arms around his neck, it might—it could just mean that a deeper feeling for her was forming within him. And oh, the joy if that were so!

"Poor Jasper,'' he said, brown eyes glinting. "I wonder if he even guessed how soon the girl who said she loved him, and cried bitter tears when he'd gone, would be unfaithful to his so-called cherished memory? Transferring all that emotion she professed to feel for him so quickly to another man?''

As if the touch of him was unbearable, she tore away, smoothing her blouse. "I should have known, I should have remembered how little a woman means to you! A body to enjoy, to make use of then discard. You're a swine, Mr. Alexander. Do you hear?''

Leaning back negligently against the table he inclined his head in apparent agreement. His refusal to quarrel with her increased her fury—with him, with herself, with the whole world. . . . He watched her, a mocking smile curving his lips, totally unmoved.

Turning, he picked up the cassette recorder and gave it to her. ''There are accessories available to help in the playback and typing. I'll want the finished product by the end of the day.''

Alicia found that she was trembling. It was, she knew, a form of shock from which she was suffering—a result of his display of power over her body and emotions, followed by his subsequent rejection and scorn.

''Yes, Mr. Alexander,'' she answered him. ''Who are you now, Mr. Alexander? Passionate lover or refrigerated boss? Don't tell me,'' she spoke from the door, ''I can guess. I can tell you this. It'll be a long time before I act the friendly neighbor and seek out your company again.''

''Friendly neighbor,'' he drawled, indifferent to her anger. ''Is that what you were being when you came so willingly into my arms?''

ALICIA WONDERED WHY Leonard was standing in her office doorway when she arrived for work. He was facing inward, as if he thought she might be hiding behind the filing cabinet. She smiled at the thought.

At last he heard her footsteps and turned. Raising her hand in greeting as she neared him, she thought he was frowning. Wondering what had upset him, she began to speak, then saw he was smiling. He must have been wondering why she was late. A glance at her watch, however, told her that she was exactly on time.

"Want me?" she asked. "Is it anything urgent, because—" Just in time she stopped herself from saying, Because I've got urgent work to do. Heaven knew what construction he might have put on those words! With his determination to make his way up the executive ladder, he'd use anything, even surmise, as a step to the top.

"Because what?"

He was even onto that! Alicia, entering her office, swiftly invented a reason. "Because I'm keen to prove myself in my new job as the boss's secretary, just as you are in your new position in the firm." To her relief, he seemed satisfied.

Walking to her desk, she hoped Leonard would not stay long. Absentmindedly she went to open the top drawer, found that it gave a little then stopped. Of course, she hadn't unlocked it! Her hand searched in her bag, then withdrew quickly. What would Leonard have gleaned from the discovery that she was so careful with the key of her drawer that she actually took it home?

Even so he was watching.

"I—I enjoyed Saturday," Alicia said, hoping that the idle comment would distract him, It succeeded, since he answered,

"So did I. We must go for a walk together again another weekend." Alicia smiled weakly at his suggestion. "Not too far distant, I hope," Leonard added.

When Alicia's nod and sigh were followed with, "Yes, well, I must get on now," Leonard nodded and left. In the silence that prevailed, she heard movement from the larger office adjoining hers. Her eyes scanned the frosted glass of the partition. Todd was at his desk and she knew that he must have overheard the conversation.

As she stared, his blurred image rippled along the frosted glass. He was stretching across his desk, picking something up, reading it. The breadth of his shoulders, accentuated just a little by the tailored suit, fascinated her. The shape of the dark head had her eyes fixed on it. The shrill ring of her telephone had her almost hitting the ceiling.

"When you've finished gazing at the outline of the man in the next-door office," the voice said cuttingly, "I should be glad if you could spare me a few minutes." The crash was deafening.

Judging Todd's mood to be bad, Alicia thought it advisable to put in a prompt appearance. Silent but expectantly alert, she met his sarcastic gaze with a guileless smile. Impudent words trembled on her tongue but she knew it was not the time to equal his sarcasm as she would had they been on home ground.

Thick eyebrows arched as he asked, "Passing the time of day with your boyfriend?"

"Just a friendly 'good morning,' Mr. Alexander." Her smile was forced, her eyes unnaturally bright.

He opened a drawer. "I wondered when I was going to see the artificial Miss Granger again. You can turn off the affected charm. It's wasted on me." He searched in the drawer. "What was Leonard Richardson doing in your office before you arrived?"

Alicia looked as bewildered as she felt. "Was he there? How was I to know?"

"You tell me."

"If I could I would." Her voice was unintentionally

sharp, but she did not apologize. An accusation was embedded in his words and she resented it.

He extracted a small polythene bag and placed it on the desk. "There's the earpiece for the cassette recorder. Since everything recorded on that tape is confidential, you'd better use it. I want no one overhearing the technicalities."

Her fingers ran around the folded flex inside the small bag. "Why are you so suspicious of me, Mr. Alexander?"

"Did I say I was suspicious?" She did not look at him. "Could it be that you're extra sensitive on the subject?"

Was Todd right? She could not answer her own question, except—she looked at him. "That empty picture frame . . . . It's because I'm a woman, isn't it, and you don't trust any women anymore, do you? You told me so." A sparkle lighted her eyes, a provocative smile curved her mouth. "Maybe I should change my sex?"

He made as if to get up but stopped himself. "Impudent little baggage!" His gaze slid over the neat figure revealed by her dark blue simply styled dress. "If it were the time and the place, I'd show you just what your femininity does to my masculine reflexes. Now get out, get in there—" he nodded toward her office "—and get on with your work."

Still smiling, she murmured, "Yes, sir," and turned, glimpsing his narrow look.

Through the typewriter's clatter and her intense concentration, there came a rustling sound from behind her. Startled out of her wits, she removed the earpiece and swung round.

Leonard stood in the doorway. Instinctively she leaned with her arms on the typewriter, covering the paper it held. "What do you want?" she demanded, then realized the cassette recorder was still switched on. With anxious fingers she searched for the "off" switch and pressed it. By now, Leonard was beside her and his eyes were already trying to read the typed words.

Quickly she seized a folder and covered them. "What do you want?" she asked in a hoarse whisper, conscious of the seated figure visible through the frosted glass partition. "Would you please go—*go*!" Wildly her hand waved toward the other office, hoping Leonard would understand that she was trying to tell him that he could be seen from the other office.

"I'm not doing anything wrong," Leonard said plaintively and in a voice that, to Alicia's agitated mind, seemed unnecessarily loud. "I just came to tell you—"

The figure through the glass seemed to be moving jerkily, as if anger had tensed his muscles. "Look." Alicia swung around in her chair. "If you want to talk, come outside." She pulled him toward the kitchen where the coffee lady was clattering cups. "Now tell me."

Leonard shook his head as if mystified. "All I wanted to say was that I won't be free at lunchtime to eat with you, so—"

"Okay, so I'll eat alone. Thanks for telling me. Next time—" she started returning to her office "—please— well, knock or something." Leonard looked at her as if she had gone momentarily mad but shrugged and went off.

By the time Alicia had got back to her desk, the office adjoining hers was empty. Where, she wondered, had Todd gone so swiftly and silently? Into Mr. Seagar's office, probably, she answered herself. Todd had not returned by lunchtime, however, so she concluded he must have left the building.

The whole of the recorded conversation was now in typewritten form and Alicia placed the cassette recorder and typed sheets in the second drawer down, locking all three drawers.

After a quick meal of a hamburger and salad at a food bar, she wandered along the Strand and made for the Embankment. It fascinated her just to stand still and watch the world—and the water—passing by. Somehow she managed to cross the road, having waited a long time for a gap in the endless stream of vehicles. Then she leaned against the parapet, her back to the river and studied the roaring mass of traffic.

There were old-fashioned lampposts bearing carvings, people walked briskly or strolled and looked around them, like tourists. Turning she stared down at the river. Here, the Thames had been tamed by the faceless property developers. Great white multistory buildings punctuated the skyline on one side, while the other was overlooked by gray-grimed office blocks. Cleopatra's Needle seemed strangely out of place in this rushing, relentless, impersonal modern world.

A blaring police car siren dragged Alicia from her reverie. It was strident enough to make even the innocent feel guilty and it stirred within her a sense of apprehension. Walking back to the office block in which she worked, she wondered whether Todd had returned. The knowledge that his home was now only a staircase's distance from hers gave a lift to her steps.

Entering her office, she saw that Todd's was still empty. She sighed, quelling the longing to see him again, hung her jacket on the coat stand and turned to find Leonard in the doorway.

"What now?" she asked irritably. "You're haunting me!"

Leonard laughed and the sound held a quality that she had not heard in him before. It was difficult to define but there was almost a note of—triumph?

"I found exactly what I wanted," he said. "And here it is." He pointed to the clothes he was wearing. "A new suit. Do you like it?"

"Leonard." A glance was enough to see the quality and cut. "It must have cost a small fortune!"

"It did, almost. While I was about it, I bought a couple of new shirts and two pairs of shoes. Well, if you want to get to the top, you've got to dress to give the people with power confidence in you."

"All the same," she frowned, "it's going a bit far. . . ." She eyed the suit, "Unless you've just received a legacy?"

He laughed again and shook his head. "Nothing like that."

He seemed so pleased with himself Alicia was puzzled but did not pursue the subject. A glance at her watch was sufficient hint for Leonard to go and she called after him, "Excellent taste, Leonard. I hope it takes you to the top."

Halmar Seagar passed Leonard in the corridor. "Have you an appointment with royalty today, Mr. Richardson?" he asked with a twinkle. "You look smart enough for it." He winked broadly at Alicia and walked on.

At the end of the day, Alicia knocked on Todd's door. It was just a formality since she knew he would not be there. She had seen through the glass that his desk was empty. He must, she decided, have forgotten his instruction to give him the transcript of the telephone conversation. Mr. Seagar's office was deserted, too, which meant that the typed sheets would have to remain in her possession until morning. Unless—unless she took them home with her and gave them to Todd that evening?

The thought of seeing Todd again filled her with such pleasure she put the clipped sheets of paper into a folder and pushed it into her shopping bag.

Todd's car was missing from the front parking lot of the apartment. Alicia's spirits drooped, slowing her steps as they climbed the stairs. A neighbor from the other apartment downstairs called out to her and waved, commenting on the weather. Alicia answered her automatically and let herself in.

The evening dragged. All the while she listened for Todd's return, and no television program, no magazine in the world could have claimed her attention as she waited. When the effort of trying to follow plots of movies, or to lose herself in magazine short stories turned to sheer torture, she gave up and washed her hair.

Combing it through when it was dry, it fluffed around her face, emphasizing the size of her eyes and deepening their color. Since the clock told her it was time for bed, she went through her nightly routine but even so, she did not give up. As she pulled on her blue dressing gown, she heard the sound for which she had been waiting.

Picking up the folder from the entrance lobby table, she opened the main door and started down the stairs. Halfway she stopped. Todd was not alone. Standing beside him was a woman, almost his own height, carefully groomed, tastefully dressed. His type, Alicia thought, breathing unsteadily, perfectly tailored to fit in with his own life-style, organized, animated, beautiful—and no doubt eminently trustworthy.

Turning away despondently, the sound of her name stopped her. Looking down, she saw that Todd was staring up. "You want me?"

"It can wait," she answered wearily and returned with heavy steps to her parents' apartment. Replacing the folder on the table, she locked the outer door and went to bed. Sleep eluded her, however, which meant that she could not even escape into dreams. Anyway, she thought with a rueful smile, she doubted whether a dream could hold her attention any more than the television or the stories had done.

Tossing and turning, she heard the sound of laughter and the closing of doors. It was probably Todd taking his lady friend home. The words, "I'll be in touch," from Todd had her sitting up. A car reversed and drove away. A door closing echoed in the empty, impersonal entrance to the apartment building. So the lady had arrived in her own car, which meant that Todd was now alone.

The bedclothes were flung back and Alicia's feet found her slippers. She didn't care if it was one o'clock in the morning, those sheets of typewritten paper would be handed to their owner.

A tentative knock on his door brought an immediate answer, as though Todd had been waiting for her, although his welcome was anything but warm. His eyes were cooler than the night breeze that crept through the swing doors from the outside. His mouth might have been set in cement, fixed hard forever.

"What the hell do you want?" His gaze swept her, leaving frosted trails all over her slightly shivering body.

If she had not been so weary with unindulged tiredness, if her shoulders had been straight instead of sagging, she would have given him a spirited reply. As it was, she answered, "Just to give you this folder. You said to give it to you—" He pulled her into his apartment and closed the door. "To give you this at the end of the afternoon. You weren't there."

"What about Halmar Seagar?"

"He wasn't there. So I brought them home for safe-keeping."

"Very commendable." His smile was sardonic but at that hour of the night she could not work out the reason. "You've certainly got the interests of Sander Design at heart, haven't you?"

Alicia frowned at the sneer in his voice. "Yes, I have," she replied quietly. "I'd hate all these secret reports to fall into the wrong hands."

"What wrong hands?"

Flustered by his curtness, she lifted tired shoulders. She could hardly say, "Leonard Richardson's, for instance." Leonard was after promotion, nothing else. It would hardly pay him to pry into subjects that, if his interference came to light, would mean his downfall.

"You know what I mean," she said feebly, thrusting the folder at him.

He took it, opened it and flipped through the contents. "As well-typed as ever."

The words were spoken in such an uncharitable tone she hit back blindly. "Mr. Alexander hands out praise! Will you please excuse me while I faint?"

He closed the folder and looked at her, a smile shaping his mouth, his eyes half-hidden. "Thanks for the thought." His tone had softened slightly. His arm went around her waist. "Come and sit down." He led her to the couch and sat beside her, putting the folder aside.

His tie was loosened, his eyes shadowed. "You look tired," Alicia commented. "Your dinner date must have exhausted you."

Hooded eyes scanned her nightclothes, lingered on her pale cheeks and her pillow-ruffled hair. "It would take more than a meal and an evening of business talk with my accountant to exhaust me. Even you, my bewitching neighbor, would discover, if I ever loosed it on you, that my reservoir of sensual energy was sufficient to last until dawn and maybe beyond."

With a smile he watched the slow color dye her cheeks. Lazily he unfastened his tie and threw it aside, unbuttoning his shirt with one hand. The sight of his lean yet solid frame, the dark head of hair uncharacteristically ruffled, stirred her emotions unbearably.

She looked away, snapping the taut thread that had locked her gaze on to his body. He laughed softly and stretched out to grasp her chin. "Do you want me, little witch?"

She wriggled under the fire of his eyes and tried in vain to free her chin. She could not shout, as she longed to do, Yes, yes, I want you with every breathing, living part of me. Instead she used anger as a weapon.

"Your *accountant*? That sophisticated woman?"

"Believe me, her brainpower is formidable. But it's never allowed to diminish her physical attributes. She's extremely well endowed with the stuff of which casual relationships are made."

"So she's got just everything," Alicia responded disgustedly. "I *hate* women like her." Even she was surprised at the violence with which she spoke the words. She qualified hastily, "Those women—they let the side down. It's not fair on the majority who have one or the other but not both.''

He laughed and leaned toward her. ''Come nearer, Miss Granger. No, nearer still.'' His arm curved and it took all her willpower not to accept its invitation. In a moment he had bridged the gap she had left. Their bodies were touching, pressing, clinging—physical desire having overcome all restraints imposed by intellect and reason.

Now she was where her dream thoughts had taken her a few minutes before—her cheek pressed to his hard chest, her fingers spread against the sinewy roughness of him, her lips, wayward, willful, slipping around to kiss and play. There were the vibrations of a rumble of laughter followed by action on his part so swift that she was lying back pinned beneath him against the cusions even before she could calculate his intention.

Now his hands were impatient with her covering, unwrapping her dressing gown, tweaking at the satin bow at the neck of her nightdress. His fingers explored as hers had done, and as he sought and found the hammering beat of her heart, she whispered, ''No, Todd, no.''

It spurred rather than deterred, and in a skimming motion his hand had traced a burning trail across her breasts, cupping one of them and lowering his head to kiss and play as hers had done to him. Her indrawn breath was locked in her lungs as he tasted and teased and she felt the need in him grow.

''Say you want me, witch,'' he growled, his stubbled chin rough against the smoothness of her. But his lips lifted and dropped, finding her mouth, leaving his stroking, tormenting hand where it was. Even if she had wanted she could not have talked. Her brain was misted like gold-tinted clouds at sunrise. She strove to please him in every way she knew, parting her moist lips and clutching at his head, unknowingly pressing his mouth into even more intimate contact.

Leaving her mouth, he trailed her cheek, her throat, her shoulder and she cried out, "I want you, Todd, I want you." Then more softly, "I love you, Todd. Do you hear me?"

He did not answer, his mind and body too absorbed in discovering, roaming and arousing. By now she had been freed of her dressing gown. Her nightdress had slipped down, revealing more to him than she had ever allowed any man to see. Beyond caring, she was ready to do whatever he asked of her. Her head moved against the cushion and she moaned, "I love you, I want you."

"Will you marry me?" The question came thickly.

Alicia grew still, her mind dazed, her body throbbing. "What did you say?" she whispered incredulously.

More clearly now he said, "Will you be my wife?"

CHAPTER SEVEN

BEWILDERED, she put a hand to her head. He hated women, he mistrusted women. "Why?" she asked. "Why?"

His eyes burned into hers. "Answer me, woman. Will you marry me?"

Her dry tongue slipped uselessly over kiss-bruised lips. "Why, Todd, when you said you—"

"You love me. Didn't you just say so? Or was it in the heat of the moment and you didn't even know what you were saying?"

"No, no, I do love you, Todd. For a long time—" Just how long had he been paying her attention? "I can't remember when. Even before you noticed me, even when I was friendly with Jasper, you were important to me. Then . . . ." She shook her head, still dazed. "Then it turned to love." Her smile was weak. "My chemistry and yours—it mixed, then flared up." He did not smile with her. "I've never let a man . . . never *loved* a man before you—"

"So you'll marry me, Alicia." It had become a demand, not a question.

"But Todd, are you sure *you* know what you're saying?" It was foolish to ask. He was not part of the sunrise as she had been before he broke the spell. He'd been down here on earth, feet on the ground, all the time of the lovemaking.

"I know what I'm saying," he replied as she knew he

would. Joy leaped, her hands gripped his shoulders, now uncovered. Yet there was something wrong, wasn't there, something missing? No joy in his eyes, no shining happiness? Maybe men felt this way? So many questions, all the answers missing.

An impatient shake of her shoulders brought the words stumbling, faltering, to her lips. "Yes, yes, Todd. I'll marry you."

Had his brown eyes hardened just a little? Not much, a mere flicker of a look? She must have imagined it, because her mouth was engulfed by his and he was draining the love from her, into him. . . .

The telephone rang. He cursed, against her lips, saying, "Let it ring." In the end, he broke away.

Her wide eyes watched him move from her. "At this time of night, Todd?"

"Could be the research lab. It's happened before. If they're onto something, they don't let a little thing like sleep worry them."

"Or other people's," she sighed, pushing at the cushion and lowering her head. Already she was missing Todd's warmth, Todd's passion, feeling deprived. . . .

Her eyes closed and she heard Todd say, "So soon? When did you get the information? Around midnight? My God, the swine's hot on the trail." This was said with sarcasm, and received with laughter that was clearly audible to Alicia as she lay dreamily on the couch.

The rest of Todd's conversation was lost as she slipped into a light sleep. When the feather-light touch of a tweaked curl woke her, she opened her eyes, blinking at the brightness of the light.

Todd was staring down at her, hands on his hips. The

set of his lips told her that the lover had gone. She asked anxiously, "Did I dream it, Todd, or did you ask me to marry you?"

"I asked you. And you accepted." He bent down and lifted her. "Bed for you." His lips brushed her briefly. "Your bed, not mine."

Frowning, she curved an arm around his neck for support. "If you want to change your mind—"

His smile left his eyes untouched. "I don't want to change my mind."

A nudging anxiety pushed its way into her thoughts. Where had the passionate man of ten minutes ago disappeared to? As he carried her up the stairs to her own home, her arms clung to his neck, her head felt the strong muscles just below his shoulder.

As he lowered her onto her bed she said earnestly, "You still don't trust me, do you?"

"Don't I?" His arms folded across his chest and his gaze ran over her disordered nightclothes.

"No. It's obvious you still haven't got over your ex-finacée's rejection of you."

"Let's get it straight once and for all. *I* did the rejecting."

He sounded so bitter, Alicia burst out, "So you've proposed to me out of a twisted kind of revenge."

His face hardened. "Is that what you think?"

She stirred, shutting out his cold eyes. "I'm so tired, Todd, I don't know what to think."

There was a brief silence and out of curiosity she opened her eyes. He was still gazing down at her. "Got a spool of thread?"

"Yes. Why? There's one over there in the drawer."

As he searched and found it, he answered, "I'm buying

you a ring." He broke off a length of thread. "I believe this is the usual way of measuring a finger size when there's nothing better around."

"Can't we go together to get the ring?" Even now it all seemed a dream.

"If I didn't have to be out of the office for the next few days, I'd say yes. But—" He measured, tying a knot, then he smiled. "You'll have to trust my judgment of your taste in jewelry."

"I don't mind if you don't give me a ring." *I do mind*, she reproached herself, *very much*.

Her statement seemed to displease him, but he did not comment. She reached up and caught his shoulders. "Must you go, Todd? I'll miss you while you're away."

"Will you?" He sat cornerwise on her bed and scooped her into his arms. With a roughness that took her completely by surprise, his hands invaded the untied neckline of her nightdress and for the second time that evening, she felt the arousing touch of his hands, his searing kiss of the yielding softness of her body.

Why, she wanted to ask him, did his eyes seem to burn with anger? Why did his mouth hit hers so hard the pain made her wince and try to twist away? The more she showed her distress the more demanding his kiss became—and, she found to her horror, the more passionate was her response to him.

"Don't leave me tonight!" Even as the whisper left her swollen lips, he pulled away and stood up, hooking his thumbs into his slacks waistband, his breathing quickened. "Don't look at me that way," she whispered, paling under his sardonic gaze. "I'm going to be your wife. You asked me, just now. So . . . so why are you condemning me for—'' she looked down at herself ''—for lying here like this, letting you see where you kissed me?'' Still his eyes taunted, and she persisted, ''Should I cover myself up, then? I—I don't know the rules of the game. Tell me, Todd.''

With one hand she closed her nightdress. With the other she reached out to touch him, but he moved away.

''Good night, my passionate fiancée. May your dreams be sweet—but most of all, untroubled.''

There was a meaning hidden in his words. ''What do you mean?'' she called after him, but her only answer was the quiet closing of the apartment door.

ALL DAY, AS SHE WORKED, Alicia was tortured by thoughts of where Todd had gone. Was he spending the whole day with his accountant, having a working lunch with her, then this evening, wining and dining her and later still . . . .

Staring across her narrow office to the gray-painted wall opposite, she found she still could not grasp that she was Todd's fiancée. After all the derogatory remarks he had made about women's faithlessness—that he would take anything a woman gave but would never offer marriage in return. . . . The question went around in her head, ''Why me? *Why me?*''

Mr. Seagar's words came back to her, ''He likes his freedom to choose, use and discard.'' She studied her engagement finger, as if it already bore his ring. Soon, he'd promised, it would be there. Wasn't that action—the giving of such a ring—a binding act, depriving him of that freedom he seemed to value so much? Or was the whole thing merely a matter of spending a sum of money because giving her such a significant a piece of jewelry would keep her happy, yet mean nothing to him but the right to make love to her, make her, if he wanted, completely his? After which, and she held her head, remembering her brazen invitation to him the night before, he would "discard" her like all the others?

"Have you a headache, Miss Granger?" Halmar Seagar's softly spoken words had her swinging around.

"No, no, I'm perfectly all right. I was just . . . thinking, that's all."

"Such somber thoughts they must have been!" His smile was kindly as he stood in the doorway. "In my friend Todd Alexander's absence, I've come to seek your help."

"Letters?" A notebook and pencil were in Alicia's hands at once. "Of course, Mr. Seagar."

In his office, he gave the dictating machine a gentle push. "I'll give you my letters verbally. This machine age, Miss Granger—I'll have no more part in it than I need to. Technology, science—wonderful things, until they start diminishing and disintegrating man's intellect, which they are doing right now, Miss Granger, I'm afraid. Please sit down."

Smiling at Mr. Seagar's measured outburst against the times in which they lived, Alicia sat. Mr. Seagar and his lunchtime sandwiches on a bench in the park, Mr. Seagar and his devotion to his wife—he lived in another age, she mused, maybe one that never existed except in his own mind. Happiness, contentment—if only Mr. Seagar's world could be everyone's world! Not least, she thought with a suppressed sigh, her own.

"I hear," Halmar Seagar broke into her thoughts, "I have to congratulate you."

Surprise brought her eyes to his. Had he heard? If so, who had told him?

"Don't look so alarmed, my dear. Todd called me before he went off to the Sander Design lab."

So that was where he had gone! Relief that he was not with his beautiful lady accountant had her smile lighting up her face.

"Thats better." Mr. Seagar had misinterpreted relief for happiness, but did it matter? "Whatever were you worried about?" He brushed the lapels of his jacket as if freeing them of imaginary crumbs. "So Todd has chosen his bride at last, the girl he's been seeking for so long. Someone to put in his picture frame, and he could hardly have picked a prettier, more worthy life partner!"

That picture frame. Alicia had a terrible feeling that it would never be her face that would one day occupy it, but the reason for her fear escaped her entirely. She only knew it was there. Smiling again and thanking Mr. Seagar for his congratulations, she waited patiently for him to dictate the first letter.

When the working day was over, she realized that she had not once seen Leonard. At lunchtime she had looked for him but the others told her he had gone out. She guessed that now he had an office of his own, he was indulging his preference for his own company. It was also likely the new design work that Todd had allocated to him was keeping him absorbed.

Leaving the office building, Alicia walked in the direction of the subway. There was a tap on her shoulder. Startled, she turned to see Leonard puffing after running to catch up to her. "Are you in a hurry?" he asked, hope giving an unusual animation to his features.

About to refuse, her heart was touched by the plea in his eyes and she shook her head. People hurrying home brushed past them impatiently and Alicia knew they would have to move. "What do you want?" she asked more irritably that she intended.

"Can we find somewhere to have a cup of coffee?" Leonard suggested. "I wanted to catch you before you left but missed you."

Alicia looked around her. "There's a café back there." She indicated a side street and Leonard joined her as they made their way toward it.

When the cups had been placed in front of them, Leonard reached in his pocket and withdrew a box. It was narrow and long with a hinged lid. "I—I thought you might like this." He spoke awkwardly, as if giving presents was not a habit of his.

Alicia looked at Leonard, her heart beating heavily. *What have I done to deserve this*, she thought and her heart started thumping, not in anticipation but in apprehension. "It's not my birthday," she commented, introducing a note of wonder into her voice and summoning up a smile.

Leonard dropped two lumps of sugar into his coffee, waiting. Waiting for the gasp that she gave at the sight of the gold necklace, with its linked squares, each engraved with a different design. A new suit, shirts, shoes, a gold necklace for her—where was the money coming from?

"But Leonard—why? It's lovely, it's beautiful, but, but . . . well, you really shouldn't. So much money and you just a—"

"I'm an engineering designer," he said, with a note of pride. "And Alexander pays me quite well now. So why shouldn't I spend my money on you? I mean, you've helped me get where I am, where I'm going in the future. . . ."

"Going where? Oh, you mean your career. I haven't helped you really, have I, Leonard? You demanded an interview with the boss, you talked him around by letting him know how much faith you had in your abilities."

Even as she fed his pride, talking persuasively to shift the responsibility for his upgrading from herself to him, her mind was asking, how have I helped him? But there was no one, nothing, no flash of intuition to give her an answer.

"It's beautiful, Leonard, and I really do appreciate your thought, but honestly, I can't. . . ." It was no use—she just couldn't say, "I'm an engaged woman now." Her engagement to Todd seemed even less real that it had that morning.

"Don't return it, Alicia. It would be an insult if you did, and people like me don't like insults. Even though Alexander's given me work that takes account of my real ability, he did it very unpleasantly, and . . . and insultingly."

Alicia shook her head, saying nothing. There was nothing she could say that would change the established thought patterns of a young man such as Leonard, whose mind must have been corroded way back in his chilhood, and who carried forever the proverbial chip on his shoulder.

"Put the necklace on, Alicia." He seemed an eager young man now, anxious to see the fruits of his efforts to better himself in their proper place.

If she complied, Alicia knew it would be tantamount to accepting the gift. She reached up and fastened the catch. As she did so, a flashlight momentarily blinded her. Leonard had taken a picture of her putting on his present!

"Hey!" She was worried now. "Why did you do that?"

Her worries were laid to rest by his answer. "So I can gloat about my success and gaze at the visible evidence of my higher status in life. I'd have bought you a ring, only— "His actions in replacing his camera in its case were overly meticulous. "I knew you'd never go for a man like me. I'm a loner."

Her hand reached across and gripped his fingers. "I know that, Leonard. That's why I've—" She cut off the sentence. If she had continued, he would have construed her words as patronizing—and maybe even insulting!

He was there all the same. "That's why you've befriended me." He finished his coffee, pushing away the cup. "I've known that all along. And that's another reason why I bought that." He indicated the necklace. "My way of saying, 'Thank you for your friendship.' "

Again she was touched by his humility. If it was not a characteristic that was usually associated with the inflated ego he seemed to possess, then she was not at that moment prepared to question it.

"Will you come to a movie with me, Alicia? I'll see you home aferward."

"Leonard, I—" How could she refuse the mute appeal in his eyes, especially after he had given her such a valuable gift? The cleaning of the apartment, the hair washing she had planned would have to be postponed until the following evening. Todd wouldn't have returned by then, she was certain, so she nodded and he thanked her, picking up the bill.

It was late when the movie ended, not that Alicia had followed the unfolding of the plot from start to finish Her mind had wandered, wondering when Todd would come home and why he hadn't told her where he was going. Her fingers had found the necklace, tracing its varied patterns in the dark, feeling it heavy around her neck, wishing Leonard had not given it to her.

He kept his word and saw her home, right to the main entrance to the apartment house. His home was a train journey's distance and he assured her it would not take him long to get there. To Alicia's relief, he demanded nothing in return for his gift or for the evening meal and the cost involved in watching the movie from the cinema's most expensive seats.

Preparing for bed, Alicia wished she had asked Mr. Séagar for the telephone number of Sander Design. If she had known, she could have called Todd. He might just have been there, even though it was almost midnight. After all, the call that had interrupted them last night—no, she corrected herself, it was this morning—had come in the early hours.

Sighing, she pulled the bedclothes over her. How many hours before she would see him again? And would he give her an engagement ring, as he had promised?

AT LUNCHTIME NEXT DAY, Alicia pushed into her bag the packet of sandwiches she had made before leaving for work. Todd's absence had left a void and she had decided to break with routine in an effort to turn her mind away from dwelling so much on him.

It meant escaping quickly from the building and avoiding Leonard. This she succeeded in doing and she made her way to the Embankment Gardens. Finding an empty bench, she sat on it and watched the birds scatter to an overhanging tree. They were, she knew, waiting to swoop on the crumbs that she, or any other people, might scatter.

After only two bites of her first sandwich, the daydream she had drifted into was interrupted by a voice saying quietly, "Have you any objections to my joining you, Miss Granger?"

It was Halmar Seagar and he was lowering himself beside her, having taken her acquiescence for granted. She told him she was pleased to have his company. To her surprise, she realized she was speaking the truth. For a long time she had felt the need to unburden herself about her problems—problems that, until that night when Todd had proposed, she did not even know she had.

"I've taken a leaf out of your book," she offered, laughing, indicating her sandwich packet. "I think I must be trying to acquire your peace of mind and contentment by lunching here."

Mr. Seagar laughed, reaching in his pocket for his sandwiches. He unwrapped the paper and rested back against the bench.

"Are you missing Todd?" The question came bluntly as Halmar's first bite had been swallowed.

Alicia took another triangle of sandwich from her packet. It gave her the time she needed to calm herself after the question's impact. At last she said, "Yes," then started eating again.

"It's only natural," Halmar stated, ignoring the crumbs dropping onto his suit. The birds chirped expectantly in the trees. There was a pause while each ate in silence. Then Halmar Seagar commented, "But the worry I caught in your face as I approached this seat is not. Nor is your search for the 'peace of mind' you mentioned just now. A newly engaged woman should be on top of the world."

This man, Alicia knew instinctively, was a friend. He,

more than anyone, seemed to believe in her. At the moment that she took a breath to pour out her troubles, Mr. Seagar said, glancing at her, ''That's a very attractive gold necklace you're wearing?''

He had spoken the statement as a question, and as such it required an explanation. Should she tell him with the honesty that such a man deserved, ''Leonard gave it to me''? Something inside her warned that this would not be wise. The reason was not clear. Was it that it might lead people to think that she was more deeply involved with Leonard than she had claimed? Such a gift would make him appear far more than a friend.

But then she herself had not found a logical explanation for Leonard's gesture, apart from the one he had given— that of seeing, in a tangible form, some of the fruits of his efforts to gain promotion, and even more important to his manly pride, worn by a woman.

Her hesitation must have been noted by such an acute observer as Halmar Seagar. He leaned sideways, inspecting the necklace more closely. ''Each square has its own individual engraving. Surely it must have been handcrafted.'' He continued with his lunch. ''A family heirloom, maybe?''

He was waiting, she knew, for a denial. Such an obviously modern piece of jewelry could not have been in any family for the decades he had implied. Was he, perhaps, giving her a way out? Or was it a test of integrity?

It hurt her almost physically to have to lie to this man. ''Yes, yes,'' she answered quickly. ''It belongs to my mother, now. But she's abroad with my father so I thought she wouldn't mind if I—''

''Isn't it a little risky to wear such a valuable thing to work?''

He was right, but she had decided to put it on that morning, knowing that with Todd's absence from the office, there would be no awkward questions from him. It would show Leonard that she appreciated his gift. Most of all, it would boost his ego and make him feel his purchase of the present had been worthwhile.

Swallowing the last piece of her lunch, she replied, "I— I liked it so much I just wanted the . . . the feel of it around my neck."

He nodded and appeared to lose interest, brushing the crumbs from him. With a smile in his voice, he invited the birds to come down from the trees and eat their fill.

One by one they swooped to peck and pick at the crumbs. They appeared to have no fear of human beings, having been tamed through the years by the close and frequent contact. Alicia watched them, too, smiling with Mr. Seagar, but still feeling uncomfortable inside at having been forced to lie to him.

"These reports I gave you to type this morning," Halmar Seagar said suddenly, "are they finished?"

"I have a few more pages to do."

"Where have you put the typed pages?"

"In my desk drawer, which is locked." She frowned "Why, Mr. Seagar?" When he did not answer, she glanced at him, seeing his preoccupied expression. "You're beginning to sound like Todd." Mr. Seagar smiled, but his eyes did not crinkle at the corners as they usually did. "He—he doesn't trust me, Mr. Seagar."

Now, taking her by surprise, it was spilling out, quite without warning. "Even though he's proposed to me, I still can't believe I'm going to marry him," she said, her voice strained. "He's said so often that women can't be trusted, that he'd never marry, but would take whatever he could get from a woman without marriage. So what did his proposal mean?''

''It means Todd loves you and wants to make you his wife.''

She shook her head slowly. ''It's not true, Mr. Seagar. I only wish it were. All the hints he's dropped about . . . about my not being trustworthy—''

''Don't you know, my dear?'' Halmar's voice was gentle.

''Know what?'' she asked anxiously.

''All these reports you've been given to work on— they've all been leaked.''

Alicia paled, clutching the bench with both hands and staring at her companion. ''Leaked? You mean—to another company?''

Halmar nodded. ''Every single one.''

''And,'' she whispered now, ''Todd suspects me?'' Halmar's stillness, his eyes studiously gazing at the squabbling birds, provided the answer. ''Where had the information been going to, Mr. Seagar?''

''You don't know?'' She shook her head fiercely. He frowned. Did even he doubt her now? If only she hadn't lied about the necklace! ''To a rival company. We've heard via the grapevine.''

''So they're starting research on the same thing? Which means they might well catch up to Todd's company and even . . . even get there first?''

''That is always a possibility,'' Mr. Seagar said seriously.

''But I don't understand, Mr. Seagar.'' Alicia gathered her things and clutched her bag. ''If Todd suspects me, then why did he ask me to marry him?''

''That's a question you'll have to ask him, my dear.''

"Mr. Seagar—" She stopped, afraid of the answer she might receive to her question. Taking a steadying breath she continued, "Mr. Seagar, do *you* trust me?"

Involuntarily, it seemed, his eyes went to the gold necklace. Then he sighed. "Deep down, I think I do believe in your honesty."

"Only *think*, Mr. Seagar?"

His shoulders lifted and fell as if he were trying to shake off a burden of doubt. "Todd warned me, after I gave you the first secret report, what a good actress you were."

"Good actress?" That night he took her to his hotel room, gave her dinner, took her home. The day or so that followed, when she had deliberately tried to mislead him about her true personality. . . . If only she had known then what damage she had been doing, and what lay before her and how it would affect his trust in her!

Now she knew the situation—that Todd suspected she had been passing on his secrets—she could not continue with their engagement. Like a roar of thunder through her head, Todd's words came back to her the day she wandered into his office at home when he was out of his apartment. "Spying on my company's research project?" he'd said.

CHAPTER EIGHT

THE TELEPHONE RANG as Alicia washed the breakfast dishes next morning. She had passed a restless night and the noise of the persistant ringing had her heart hammering. Her dread that the caller might be Todd had her drying her hands without too much haste. Yet there was a longing inside her to hear his voice. In the end she ran to the phone.

"Alicia?" The familiar voice had her pulse rate speeding.

"Speaking. Todd?" Even now she could not keep the eagerness from her voice. "Are you . . . are you well?"

"As well as can be expected," came the dry reply. "I called you to tell you not to go into the office this morning. Take the main-line train from London to Hertford. I'll meet you there and take you to the research lab."

Alicia said she understood, yet she could not believe what her ears had heard. After all that Mr. Seagar had told her about Todd's suspicions being centered on her, he was calmly proposing to allow her to see the laboratory where the research was actually taking place.

With a stab of dissapointment, she saw that it was not Todd who had come to meet her. A young man was hovering. He approached and asked, "Miss Granger of Alexander Autoparts and Components?" Alicia nodded and he held out his hand. "I'm Sam Bridgewater, Sander Design. Todd sent me to meet you. Sent his apologies, too."

Alicia smiled and said she understood, which she didn't,

but told her heart to stop sinking and stay right were it ought to be. The car journey took them away from the city buildings and the residential areas to open counrty. They passed villages with the occasional thatched house, ancient half-timbered buildings and leafy lanes leading past them.

The conversation had been general; about the weather, the economy and what the future might hold. The driver halted the car outside a whitewashed cottage with a red-tiled roof that, here and there, curved with age. It was, the young man explained, two cottages knocked into one. Inside, he said, helping Alicia out of the car and locking it, the walls had been removed, making it into one long building.

It came as no shock, therefore, to see as she entered, that all sense of homeliness had been swept away. The area had been converted into a laboratory—the research lab of which Todd had spoken. From across the room he smiled, but he did not walk over to greet her. So, she thought, in this place, which was his first love—as Mr. Seagar had implied—she was the boss's secretary, his proposal of marriage apparently forgotten.

A voice came from across the room. "Come over here, Miss Granger, my darling."

Alicia stared at him, wondering if he was aware of what he had said. He was supremely aware, judging by his faintly derisive look. The others, it seemed, had been astonished by the command with its added endearment.

"You'd better go," one of the young men said, smiling broadly, "when your master's voice says, 'come.' "

Every eye was upon her as she made her way around chairs and benches and put her fingers into Todd's impatiently outstretched hand. He drew her to his side and looked down at her, every inch of him the adoring fiancé. Except, and the omission to Alicia was glaring, he had not, apparently, told his employees that he was engaged to her.

If he had, they wouldn't be staring as if they couldn't believe their eyes. So where did that leave her? In the undignified position of being his latest in a long line of women. Was this his way of hitting out at her for what he suspected she was doing? Her flushed face rose to his, her eyes glowering, her pouting lips rebellious. His maddening response was to throw back his head in laughter, then put his lips lightly to hers.

"Do we hear wedding bells?" Sam Bridgewater asked with a smile.

Todd answered lazily, "You know my opinion of weddings."

"Do we not," someone commented. "Take care, Miss Granger. Our boss with the roving eye doesn't believe in marriage."

Alicia smiled, her lips as taut as her stomach muscles.

Todd went on and it was as if he were taunting her, "Who needs marriage when women are so willing these days to dispense with the ceremony and give a man—"

Unable to stand his spiteful repartee, Alicia jerked away, but he pulled back. "Don't go, my love. I've got some work for you. But first I'll show you around the lab."

"You're honored, Miss Granger," said a bearded young man whose name, Tony, was printed on his T-shirt that showed underneath his white coat. "Everything in this building is top secret, totally confidential—"

"And incomprehensible to anyone without scientific knowledge," Sam added with a grin.

Alicia laughed, liking the relaxed atmosphere and the

alert, dedicated young men employed there. But, she told herself with a secret smile, she liked their employer even better!

With his arm around her waist, Todd guided her around the extensive laboratory. They passed walking-height counters with high stools placed at intervals. There was a storeroom leading off for glassware and beakers. The windowsills were cluttered with empty coffee mugs and beer and coke cans. Some of these had spilled over onto the floor.

Next to a blackboard was a white board, covered in handwritten chemical formulas. This puzzled Alicia and she commented, "How can white chalk show up on that?"

"Ah," Todd answered "we use felt-tipped pens of different colors. We discuss ideas, and variations of those ideas. We write—say, something like this," he picked up a green pen and wrote a formula with lightening speed—which, Alicia knew by experience, was how his brain worked. "Then we take a rag dipped in cleaning fluid, rub out the writing and start again."

His arm was around her shoulders now. "Here," he explained, moving her to a bench, "is a continuous experiment. It's watched all the time and measurements are taken."

"It's never switched off?"

"Never." He whispered against her ear. "Like me from you."

"Now then, Todd," said the bearded Tony from the other end of the laboratory, "wait until you're alone, can't you?"

Todd laughed with his employees and, in spite of her irritation at his familiar attitude, Alicia laughed, too. It pleased her to see that here, in the place that Mr. Seagar had called Todd's pride and joy, Todd dropped his autocratic manner and was completely at one with the young men who worked for him. It occurred to her that he must trust them all implicitly—far more than he trusted her!

"Come into my office." He caught her hand and drew her toward an ancient wooden door that had plainly been preserved when the alterations had been made. "This work I mentioned. It's urgent."

As he closed the door, there were calls of, "Watch it, Todd," and, "Remember, it's work, not play, you're going to do!" Todd smiled good-naturedly. When the door had creaked shut, a frown replaced the smile. The arm around Alicia's shoulders dropped away. Glancing at him in an effort to discover even a hint of the warmth he had displayed while with his colleagues, she discovered that his eyes and his mouth had hardened and that his entire expression seemed to be coated with the usual layer of frost.

"Why," she challenged, "didn't you tell them we were engaged? Why did you let them believe we were having a secret affair?"

"Maybe because—" his sarcastic gaze derided "—I'm a secretive person. Unlike some . . . people I know." The slight hesitation had been deliberate, Alicia was sure.

He motioned her across the room. Once it had been a living area. The low beams remained. There was a wide, open hearth and fireplace that had been preserved and in the opening of which had been constructed an iron grate complete with logs. Its feeling of history lived on, defying twentieth-century man's efforts to eliminate it.

A desk stood under a diamond-paned window. A typewriter was on the desk, a typist's chair waited to be occupied. Alicia stood uncertainly by it, swiveling it slightly with her left hand, awaiting instructions. When they came, they took her breath away.

"Give me your handbag."

Wide eyes swung to Todd's and she gripped the bag more tightly. "Why?"

"This work I'm about to dictate is top secret. Like the laboratory itself, not a single bit of description of it must be passed on."

He prized the bag from her fingers. "And you don't trust me," she said flatly.

"I don't trust you."

She drew in her lips, compressing them until they hurt. She would not plead for his trust. "Is that—" Her breath caught, but she persisted. "Is that why you haven't bought me an engagement ring?"

He was opening her bag. "I haven't had time," he dismissed, as if the matter was of little consequence. After what Mr. Seagar had told her, she was sure that Todd never would buy her a ring. His proposal had been a joke, a beautiful—and terrible—joke!

The bag's contents lay scattered on the desk. Todd inspected every item, even the lipstick.

"What are you doing?" she ask, appalled. "What do you think I've got in there?"

"Who knows? Bugging devices come in all shapes and sizes these days."

"Bugging devices?" She whispered the words in horror, feeling ill that his mistrust of her went so deep. "Do you honestly believe that I'm capable of betraying you in that way?" She would tell him the truth even if he didn't believe her. "Todd." She put her hand on his arm, staying its movement. "I—I love you. How could I let down the man I love?"

"Those sentiments mean nothing to me. I've heard them before." His jaw was rock hard and he shook off her hand, throwing the empty bag back to her. "Okay, I've cleared that."

Indignant at having to replace her own belongings, she scooped them back with bad grace. As she snapped the bag shut, his next words froze her to the spot.

"Right, it's your turn now."

The blood drained from her cheeks. "You don't mean . . . strip?" He folded his arms and gave one impatient nod. His eyes glinted like steel and she felt he was boring holes through her head. Her panic rose. "You said that once before, Todd, but you didn't mean it." He was like a statue. "You—you just can't be serious now."

"I'm deadly serious. This lab, the work it's doing, is so secret that if one word gets out about what we're doing here, we'll have lost everything, our backers, our funds, our lead over other companies working on similar lines."

Was he saying all this, Alicia wondered, to underline just how contemptibly she had acted in passing on, as he thought, the contents of those secret reports she had worked on?

"Worst of all," he continued relentlessly, "we would have lost the race to be first. And that, my beautiful—" Alicia started to back away "—would jeopardize the nation's chance to gain a first in the field. Worth making sure, don't you think, that Sander Design isn't lumbered with an industrial spy who steals its secrets and deprives it of its precious and hard-won lead? So . . . ." He lifted his hand.

"Go into that walk-in closet and remove your jacket and whatever else you're wearing."

Immobilized by dread, plus the belief that he did not really mean what he was saying, she could only stare, white-faced.

"Or . . . ." He advanced slowly, arms still folded. "Do you want me to tear the clothes from you? Which—" as she retreated "—as your future husband, I have every right to do."

"Future husband. . . ." The words sounded as strange and unacceptable as the nightmarish circumstances. Still facing him, she found the closet door by feeling behind her with her hands. Opening the door she backed in. He followed, standing in the doorway.

Trying desperately to deflect him from his purpose, she said, "But, Todd, I don't understand. You've let me see—and type—secret documents many times. You've never taken these precautions before. So why now?"

His lips firmed. He chose not to answer, and she knew she had to obey. With her eyes riveted on his, she moved as if she were hypnotized. First her jacket came off. He picked it up, and as she slowly unbuttoned her blouse, he continued to look at her. She could not tear her eyes from his. Nor could she even think. It was possible only to feel, to experience the slow throbbing of her body, the heavy hammering of her heart, the way her lungs were functioning shallowly.

Even as he felt inside the jacket pockets, then dropped the garment down, he held her eyes. "Now the blouse," he ordered quietly.

The words brought her mind back to life. "I refuse. You can't make me."

His hands were on his hips now, his feet placed slightly apart. "Can't I?" he grated.

Only too well she knew he could. "You're no better than a rapist," she spat at him.

His hooded eyes seemed to be taking the measure of her. "The more you resist my request to allow me to search you, the more I suspect you've got something to hide."

"*Request*? It was an order, and I don't obey orders from men like you." It was a losing battle, but she would not be bettered without a fight. "You have no search powers, and I have my rights as a citizen—"

"I have my rights as your husband-to-be." He moved so swiftly he was peeling off the blouse before she could stop him.

"You're miserable, you're a low-down, hateful devil."

He was examining the blouse pocket, which was empty. He threw it down on to the discarded jacket. "Now the bra."

"Not on your life!" she flung at him and made a dive for the blouse. He was there, gripping her wrist and jerking her against him. Her breasts lifted and fell against his chest, her eyes blazed into his. His jaw gritted, then his mouth dropped onto hers, dropped like a rock falling, grinding her lips against her teeth—until it came to her through the pounding of her blood that if she yielded, as her body now clamored to do, if she melted into him, he too might soften and drop his demand.

By now he had forced her lips apart and, with even reason abandoned, to be replaced by a quivering emotion, she permitted and gloried in his possessive exploration of the moist responses within. His palms moved feather-light over her shoulders, down, down to her hips, pulling her harder against him.

Then his hands slid upward, seeking and cupping her breasts. She moaned as the touch of this man's hands aroused her deepest emotions, causing her to forget the circumstances, the time, the place. Anything he asked of her, she told herself feverishly, she would do. She swayed and clung, kissing him back again and again.

In the moment that they broke away, on her part to regain her breath, she discovered that her bra was gone and that it was there in his hands. Swiftly he examined it, using fingers and eyes, then threw it to join the pile.

"Why, you miserable, rotten—" She crossed her arms in front of her, breathing as though she had been running. "And I thought you'd changed your mind, that you were kissing me because . . . because you loved me. I should have known how hard you are, and how you regard women."

Lifting a hand, he ran it over his hair. "My God, you have a potent effect on a man." He loosened his tie, his eyes never leaving her. There was a narrow look in them that told her he was still not satisfied with his investigations. "Has that skirt got pockets? No? Let me feel."

Covering herself as she was, she could not prevent his hands from sliding over her hips and thighs, but she came back fighting. "Maybe you'd like to look in my shoes, or my hair."

"I was coming to that." The mouth that only moments before had plundered hers had become a thin line. "Step out of your shoes."

Without removing her crossed arms, she did as he asked. He picked up each shoe, searching it thoroughly, examining the heels, and tapping them. Then he gave them back. "Please put them on the floor," Alicia requested, attempting to sound imperious. He continued to hold them out, eyes glinting with something near to devilry. She had no choice but to move an arm and take them. He put only one into the outstretched hand, holding onto the other. His smile conveyed the message, "Checkmate."

Infuriated, she lifted the shoe she held and lunged at him with it. He stepped aside and grasped her other arm, jerking it from its protective hold and pushing the second shoe into her hand. Then he held her wrists apart, looking her over, with excrutiating thoroughness. Slowly he bent, still keeping her arms opened wide, and placed lingering kisses on each pink-tipped breast.

Her legs were weakening, her heart racing. "You have no right to be doing this, Todd. I came in here to work—"

He dropped her arms and the frost in his eyes to which she had grown so accustomed drove out the devilish glint. Involuntarily she shivered. "Now I'm satisfied that you're carrying no bugging device, we'll get down to that work."

Again she dived for her clothes. This time he allowed her to dress, but still he watched her, his expression unreadable, his emotions entirely under control. Hers, on the other hand, were in a turmoil and every instinct urged her to throw herself into his arms, begging for his kisses.

In her confusion, she fumbled at her bra fastening. Maddened by his broad smile, she turned her back on him—then realized her mistake. She shivered as his fingers made contact with her skin, but this followed at once by a flame of anger as he drawled, "It's not my usual custom to dress a woman after she's undressed for me, but . . . ." His hands slid around to cup her shape. "I'll make an exception for you."

At last he had finished and she was dressed again. "I have never," she stormed, "ever, been so humiliated in my whole life. Consider our engagement a thing of the past. I never believed you meant what you said, anyway, in asking me to marry you."

"I meant it, Alicia. I intend to make you my wife." He spoke each word slowly and clearly. "Do you understand?"

"No." She picked up her bag. "I've turned deaf. And I'm leaving, right now."

His hand shot out and caught her wrist, jerking her back from the door into the main office. "You're staying, right here with me. There's work to be done. This was part of it. You're a security risk, my darling. I had to make sure."

"Don't desecrate that lovely endearment by using it on me. You don't mean a word of it." Todd followed her into the office, and she turned to face him.

"Why am I a security risk? Why? And why do you suspect it's me who's passing on information? Mr. Seagar told me . . . ." She might as well be talking, she thought sadly, into a disconnected telephone. "Couldn't it be someone else?"

"Here's the typewriter," he said, ignoring her questions. "It's an old model but it works. I'll dictate, you type. Right? Any complicated formulas or technical terms I'll write with chalk on the board." It was, she discovered, a specially adapted typewriter for typing mathematical terms, which made her work easier. All the time, except for writing on the blackboard—and even that was at an angle so that he could see every movement she made—his attention was on her. His scrutiny fed her simmering anger, making her fingers trip and stumble over the keys. He tutted her errors but she did not say, "It's your fault."

Apart from his ego-reducing search of her clothes and the ensuing intimacy between them, he had remained the aloof employer. His whole manner placed an embargo on any form of familiarity. When the dictation was finished, he watched her gather up the sheets of paper and clip them together, then took them from her.

He showed her the ladies' washroom where she could tidy herself, then led her from the building through another exit door. "I'll drive you to the station," he said, showing her into his car.

"Go straight home," he instructed, as they arrived in the station.

"Aren't you coming, too?" Any words would do, she thought, desperately, to bridge the awesome gap that seemed suddenly to have formed between them.

"I'm booked into a nearby hotel for a few nights. So . . . no, I won't be coming home with you."

He left her at the station and drove away at once. *Some engagement*, she thought miserably as she watched his car pass out of sight. *Some fiancé . . . some lover he would be!*

Then she looked at her empty hand and remembered that he "had not had time" to buy the ring. If they ever did marry, she knew that, although he would play the lover, he would never give her the love she craved.

CHAPTER NINE

IT WAS FRIDAY afternoon and the end of a week that had seemed to be without end. Alicia had eaten her midday meal that day with Leonard and he had asked her why she was not wearing his necklace.

She had laughed and told him that it was too good to wear for the office. "I keep it for special occasions."

"That means I'm not there to see it," he had objected.

His answer had rather shocked Alicia. It had, she thought, bordered on conceit and vanity. But that, she reminded herself, was the only reason he had given her the necklace in the first place.

Arriving home weary and despondent, she let herself into her parents' apartment, dropping her bag onto a chair. The crunch of car wheels swinging around in the front parking lot had her listening intently and wishing the thud of her heartbeats did not make so much noise. Running out onto the landing, she saw a man push through the doors—and stare right into her eyes.

"Todd!" she greeted him, her whole face alight with pleasure, and she started down the stairs. Then she recalled how distantly they had parted and her smile dissolved into a frown. Cursing her own impetuosity, she retreated upward toward her own apartment. For a few seconds he stood gazing up at her. Then he took the stairs two at a time.

Quickly she backed through the entrance door and closed

it, but before the lock could click shut, his shoulder was to the door. Slowly, easily he overcame her weaker pressure and the door moved irrevocably open. A final push had her stumbling backward. While she regained her balance, Todd came in, leaned against the closed door, arms folded.

"So I'm not welcome?" Brows lifted sardonically. "The joyful greeting was for someone else, but it turned out to be me?"

There was no way of preventing her horrified reaction. 'That's not true! I knew it was you, but . . . ." She walked across the entrance hall into the living room. He followed. Turning, she faced him. "But I haven't forgiven you for . . . for that order to strip you gave me at your research lab."

His head went back in laughter. When he had recovered from the joke against her, he dwelt thoughtfully on the anger that simmered in her eyes. Slowly he removed his jacket. "Would you like to have your own back?" he queried, his hand going to his tie. Under her wondering eyes he removed it and started unfastening his shirt buttons. "Shall I strip for you?"

There was devilment in his eyes and she knew that in a few moments, unless she acted, he would be standing before her. . . .

"No!" she shrieked and dived forward, matching buttons to buttonholes. Fists on hips, his smile tolerant, he allowed her to continue, then he unfastened the top button again. "You can still search me," he coaxed. He caught her hands and pressed them against his chest, moving them down to his waist and his hips. Fearful of what his next action might be, and aware of the shiver of excitement that coursed through her at the leanness of his body beneath her palms, she twisted her hands from his grasp.

It seemed he was ready for her action. Moving quickly he reached out, catching her shoulders and pulling her to him. His hands slipped to find her shoulder blades beneath the material of her dress, his fingers moving to mold them until her arms closed around his neck. The kiss when it came brought a leaping flame into her limbs and it was as though, until that moment, from the moment they had parted, she had been only half alive.

When he let her go, there was a gleam in his eyes she had never seen. His full lips curved into a smile and it was as though a sunlike warmth had melted the ice that had had his emotions in its grip.

His changed attitude puzzled her. Despite the blood that now flowed swiftly, instead of sluggishly, through her veins, there still rankled inside her a deep resentment at his mistrust of her.

"Maybe *I'm* the one who's forgiven?" she said with a sting. "Have you decided that, having found no listening or recording devices hidden on me the other day, that I'm not the danger to you you thought I was?"

He picked up his tie and replaced it. "I came," he said, ignoring her taunt, "to tell you that I'm giving a small party this evening, a kind of delayed apartment warming."

"You had one the day you moved in. Don't you remember? I was the only guest."

He smiled, palms on his hips under his jacket, which he had pulled on. "That was just a trial run. This will be the real thing. A few friends—"

"Don't tell me," she fenced, "you need a hostess, which is why you're asking me."

His smile had cooled. "I'm inviting you because I want you there and more important, because you're going to be my wife."

"I said I didn't want to marry you. I told you to forget it." There was a strange force inside her that was driving her on. It was as though the resentment had turned to bitterness, and it was making her say the exact opposite of the words she really wanted to speak. "How can you marry me when you don't trust women, and never will? How can you marry an industrial spy, someone who's passed on all your company's precious secrets. I've . . . I've already passed on what you dictated me at the laboratory." Her head lifted high. "Didn't you know?"

"Don't be a little fool. I've got evidence that you did no such thing."

"Oh, so I'm in the clear now, am I?" Her voice had risen and she felt ridiculously as though she wanted to cry. "And because of that, it's quite all right for you to marry me! Well, I'm not coming to your precious party. Contact your beautiful accountant. She'll act as your hostess much better than I would. What's more, you *trust* her."

Alicia turned away and made for the kitchen but hands on her shoulders spun her around. "I trust *you*, you crazy wench."

As his mouth lowered again, she spun away. "You don't, I know you don't. Mr. Seagar told me—"

He turned on his heel and she was talking to his retreating back.

IT WAS ALMOST EIGHT o'clock and she was curled on the couch watching a television movie. She was wearing her oldest clothes and breaking pieces of chocolate off a bar.

For the past hour she had done her utmost to shut out the sound of clinking glass and the clatter of crockery and cutlery. The van belonging to a firm of caterers stood in the front parking lot and she knew they were there in connection with Todd's party.

Her mouth was full of chocolate when the doorbell chimed. Alicia hesitated, chewing and swallowing hastily. She feared that it might be Todd, although after her bad-tempered refusal of his invitation, she doubted if he would renew it.

It was the fact that Leonard had mentioned that he might—just might—call on her that evening that made her uncurl herself from her comfortable position and answer the door. The moment she saw who it was, she went to slam the door in the visitor's face, but his foot was there and once again that day, Todd was forcing himself into her parents' apartment.

He looked her up and down. "Did I forget to tell you?" he asked coolly. "My party's more formal than the ones you're probably accustomed to. You have ten minutes to find more suitable clothes before the time I told the guests to arrive."

"I'm not coming to your party. I said so."

His lips tightened, his fingers dug into her shoulder and he forced her toward the bedroom. Closing the door, he stood guard, arms folded. "Look in your closet for something to wear."

"I refuse."

He detached himself from the door and her heart bounded with each one of his slow steps. He reached out and caught a wrist, captured the other and forced them behind her, putting them both into one of his hands. He pulled her

toward a closet, opened the doors and ordered, "Choose."
She closed her eyes. "Okay." The back of his hand flipped
along the garments hanging there. "This, I think."

He chose a long, pale blue gown with rope-narrow straps
and a top that started below the armpits. A back zipper held
the dress in place.

"I can't wear that," Alicia protested. "it's much too—
well, too everything for an apartment warming party. It's
meant for a much more glamorous occasion."

"I want you looking glamorous." He flung the dress
over a chair.

She wrenched free. "I told you, I won't—"

"But you will." Before she knew what he was up to,
her T-shirt was jerked over her head. Once again he was
seeing her uncovered, since she had not bothered to replace
her bra when changing from her working clothes.

"Give me back my top!" she raged, but he threw it
across the room, then moved purposefully toward her,
"Now the jeans."

Backing away, she said, "I know when I'm beaten. I'll
change. I'll put on the dress." Her arms were tightly across
her. "But you've go to get out first. I must wash, dress,
do my face."

He looked into her smoldering eyes and smiled. "If you
delay too long in coming down, or if you run out on me,
I swear I'll contact the police and register you as a missing
person."

"You've made your point," she replied, looking down
and wishing his eyes would leave her alone.

"I'm almost sorry," he said softly, "I invited people
tonight. I could be spending the evening here with a beautiful girl."

Her indignant glare amused him deeply as he asked, "How long?"

Her bare shoulders lifted. "Twenty minutes."

"Keep to it," he commanded as he went away.

TODD'S HAND came out as she stood uncertainly at his living room door. The main entrance door had been left unlocked and people were entering with the ease and familiarity of old friends.

"On time to the minute," Todd commented, smiling. "As every good secretary should be, of course. And stop giving me that 'drop dead' look." His hand gave her a playful, but in such company, embarrassing, slap.

Across the room a gray-haired man stood watching. He was tall, with a lean build despite his age, and there was a tantalizingly familiar look about his face. His well-tailored suit and ease of manner gave him the air of a successful businessman.

Todd took Alicia's hand, leading her from group to group. There were young men, with attractive women at their sides. A number of the men's faces she recognized from the Sander Design research laboratory.

With her hand still firmly held by Todd's, Alicia exchanged laughing comments with the men she had met. "What did Todd do with you the other day, Miss Granger?" a man whom she recognized as Sam Bridgewater asked. "I was expecting to take you back to the station, but he spirited you away."

"I did spirit her away," Todd replied to laughter. "Through the other exit door into my car. To the station," he added amidst knowing laughter and comments of good-humored disbelief.

"After we'd worked in Todd's office," Alicia added. "We worked hard, too, didn't we, darling?" She gave him an impish grin.

He looked her over, his eyes undisguisedly wolfish and she colored under the blatant message he was conveying to the onlookers. "*Very* hard, darling," he responded. Turning to others he said, "You know, I never knew a large closet had so many and varied uses—"

The loud laughter cut him off and there was no need for him to elaborate. Again he looked at Alicia, and saw with something like satisfaction the flash of indignation with which her eyes tried to scorch him. Once more his innuendos were leading his employees to believe that they were having an affair, which, as a result of his broad hints, was not now so very secret after all.

At the jerk of her hand—on which his grip tightened— he pulled her away to approach the older man Alicia had noticed earlier. "Alicia," Todd said, "my father, Julius. Father, this is Alicia Granger."

Now Alicia could trace the likeness that had eluded her at first sight. There was the same appraisal in the brown eyes—a lighter brown than his son's—but there was warmth, not coldness, in the older man's scrutiny.

When the introduction was over, Julius Alexander remarked, "My wife and I have heard a great deal about you. But you're even better than Todd gave us to understand." The smile that followed the words held the same charm as that of his son—when that son chose to exercise it, which, Alicia recalled, was rarely.

"My mother," Todd explained, "had a long-standing appointment for this evening."

"She was angry with Todd," Julius said, "for arranging

this—'' his hand indicated the guests ''—at such short notice. She's been wanting to meet you, too.''

How had Todd described her, Alicia wondered. As his secretary, his neighbor, or his girl friend? Never, she was sure, as his fiancée. Julius was inquiring about her parents. "Does your father work abroad permanently?'' he asked.

"He's based in London," Alicia explained, "but often goes to Europe in connection with his work. So my mother goes with him. At the moment, he's in Denmark. I think they're moving on soon to Belgium. He's in insurance," she finished, and Julius nodded.

Now and then father and son exchanged glances. It seemed that messages were passing between them, and that each understood the other. Alicia felt uncomfortably that she was the subject of those messages. What were these two silently saying to each other?

Julius bent slightly and lifted Alicia's left hand. He glanced at his son and his graying eyebrows lifted in question. This in turn gave way to a puzzled frown. A smile chased it away and he dropped Alicia's hand, turning to his son. "No ring, Todd?"

Before Todd could answer, Alicia interposed defiantly, "He hasn't had time, Mr. Alexander. He told me. But even if he had . . ..'' Now her bright eyes challenged Todd. "I told him I wouldn't become—''

Todd's narrowed regard was as effective as twin icicles dripping down her back. Mentally she shivered, awaiting the impact of the scathing words that were almost visibly hovering on his lips. "When the right time comes, father, I shall put my mark of possession on her."

Julius laughed and seeing Alicia's incensed expression, commented, "Todd has a way of—if I may say so—'' to his son "—stroking women's feelings to life with a velvet-backed glove that has a palm of sandpaper." He lifted shoulders as broad as his son's. "However, to each generation its own methods of courtship."

Alicia responded, head high, "It's old-fashioned but a good word—courtship, Mr. Alexander." Her blue eyes flared into Todd's. "Your son's methods are well known. *Choose, use and discard*—that's how Mr. Seagar described them."

"Did he now?" said Todd. "And I thought Halmar was my friend."

Julius Alexander laughed loudly. "Yes, that sounds like Halmar—blunt but subtle with it. Contented and happy, but understanding other people's troubles."

"He's a wise man," Alicia stated. "And—" she swung toward Todd "—a trusting man."

Two pairs of eyebrows rose, and father and son exchanged yet another glance. Someone claimed Todd's attention and he pulled Alicia with him. The conversation was about the research project and the young man looked uncertainly at Alicia, then at Todd.

"You can speak freely in front of Miss Granger, Des. She knows about Sander Design. And she's had no training in science, so—" with an intimate gesture he spread his hand around the back of her bare neck "—she won't understand a word."

"Sure I'm not loaded with electronic devices?" she asked overly sweetly, accepting her second drink of the evening as a girl held out a tray.

"Absolutely sure." Todd's smile held malice. "I watched you dress, remember?" The malice grew with his smile as he watched her cheeks flame. All this, she thought, in front of one of his employees! And still there was no ring on her finger.

She provoked him again. Her fingers found Leonard's gold necklace. "What about this? Surely you didn't overlook it?"

The back of his hand brushed her throat as he felt the engraved links. She held her muscles tense as she endured his touch without any outward reponse. Removing his hand, he seemed satisfied that it was safe. "No, I didn't overlook it. It's a pretty piece. Where did you get it?" His tone was bland, like his expression.

"I—I—" She would have to repeat the story she told Mr. Seagar. "It's my mother's."

"Worth a small fortune," the man called Des commented admiringly. Then his discussion with Todd was resumed.

A tray of appetizers came close and Alicia accepted one, eating it with relish. Unable to move away because of Todd's restraining hand, Alicia was forced to listen to the talk, although she did not understand a word. She wished now that she hadn't decided to wear the necklace. It had been a kind of act of defiance, although the only person who could possibly be hurt by her wearing it was herself.

A second appetizer followed the first and she looked around her fretfully. At last Todd's discussion finished and he circulated again, taking her with him.

The party ended well before midnight. Julius Alexander took Alicia's hand. Then, on a strange kind of impulse, bent to kiss her cheek. "That's from my wife," he explained, smiling. "She wanted to meet you very much."

There was an involuntary wistfulness in Alicia's voice as she said, "I've enjoyed meeting you, Mr. Alexander."

"And I you. I hope—" with a glance across the room

at his son "—it's a pleasure that will be repeated. Some years ago my son was hurt by a woman—his pride, I think, more than his heart—and he's never forgotten or forgiven.''

Alicia nodded. "He told me. But . . . years ago, you said? I thought it was only recently. You see, there's that empty picture frame.'' Julius nodded, with a smile. "Mr. Seagar said,'' Alicia mentioned quickly, noticing Todd making his way toward them, "it was a Keep Off sign to women.''

Julius laughed. "True. Until he finds the right face to fill it. I think maybe he has—''

"Has what?'' said the son in question.

"Has brains as well as looks,'' his father joked.

"Actually,'' Alicia retorted, "we were discussing what you were like as a little boy.''

Julius laughed, Todd's smile was unenthusiastic. "This,'' said Julius, "is where I tactfully withdraw from the scene. Good to have met you, Alicia.'' There was another kiss on her cheek. "You must meet my wife sometime.'' To Todd, with a sudden seriousness, "Make it soon, son.''

When he had gone, Todd commented dryly, "My father seems to have adopted you.'' With a quick scan of her flushed features, her shape, her bare arms and shoulders, he drawled, "No, cancel that statement fast.''

They were alone now and, looking at the brown eyes gazing broodingly into hers, Alicia experienced a feeling of anticlimax. What had she expected? An opening wide of his arms, herself running into them, a declaration from him of unending love?

"I wonder,'' she said to break the tense silence, and fidgeting with a shoulder strap, "that you didn't invite your lady accountant.'' She supposed she had meant to nettle him, but wished by the faint narrowing of his eyes that she had not spoken those words.

"I never mix my women."

Her smile was more despondent than tired. "I guess I asked for that." Turning to the door, she wondered how it was that the father liked her almost on sight, yet the son, whom she had known—for years, it seemed to her sighing mind—looked on her only as a specimen of womanhood, to be sampled, put to the test, then pushed aside.

"I'll see you home." He spoke behind her and she shook her head without turning, then shivered as his lips brushed her ear, whispering, "You have a long way to go."

Smiling, she shook her head, only just restraining herself from letting her head sink back against his shoulder. "There's no need, but thanks."

Disregarding her refusal of his offer, his arm went around her shoulders and, side by side, they walked upstairs. In her parents' living room, she remarked, idly repositioning the family photographs on the mantel, "Your father told me that the engagement you keep blaming for your mistrust of women happened years ago."

"It did."

"So you must have been quite a young man."

"What if I was?"

His irritated tone brought her around. "Yet you still carry on this vendetta you have against women?"

"I hadn't noticed, had you?" His eyes were trailing a path that, it was plain from his faintly lustful look, his hands would love to take.

Don't leave me tonight. . . . She recalled her cry to him the night he had proposed. Then she remembered the lack of answering emotion in his calculating examination of her features as she had lain there, feeling wanton and guilty.

"All right, you've made love to me, and . . . and I responded. But . . . but there wasn't any response in you. No warmth, no giving, like a man trying to please the woman he loves. There was . . . there was only a taking—"

He was approaching but she did not back away. "And I know why." She drew a deep breath to steady her voice. "You even warned Mr. Seagar about me, told him I was a good actress."

He was closer now, near enough for her to feel his breath warming her lips.

"Do you love me, Alicia?" he asked impatiently.

"*Desperately*," she wanted to cry out but her pride would not let her. Using sarcasm as a weapon, she answered in honeyed tones, "Oh, passionately, darling."

His brown eyes darkened with anger. "You know damned well you do. How many times have you said, 'I love you, Todd'?"

Attempting to ignore the slow throbbing of her pulses, she hit back, "If in your eyes I'm not trustworthy, how do you know that when I said I loved you, I wasn't lying?"

His anger had intensified and his hand reached out to grasp her shoulder. Nails dug painfully into her flesh but she would not beg for mercy. Inside she was weeping, despairing of ever finding that missing ingredient from their relationship—the love an engaged man should not only feel, but *show*, for his future wife.

She was pulled toward him, and the length of his hard body against her increased the tempo of her pulses. "You're trustworthy, you stupid little fool." Now both his hands possessed her shoulders and from their grip was a biting torment. "I've got proof. The report I dictated to you in the lab, and which was confined only to the lab, was not leaked to the usual source."

Now the brown eyes gleamed with something that was not anger. She gazed up at them, half afraid to accept the message they seemed to be printing out. "How do you know?" she whispered.

His smile was warmed with the expectation of the kiss that hovered on the narrowest of air currents between them. "I told you, I *know*. Be satisfied with that. I have my methods. As you, my love, will discover one day soon. . . ."

The kiss came swooping and the whole of her being seemed to be floating through space. Then she was clinging to the strength of him as if his body was as sheer as a cliff face and she was hanging perilously over a fathomless sea. Wherever his hands touched her, they gripped, arousing her as surely as a stroking palm.

His lips pulled away sufficiently for him to murmur against her mouth, "Am I *warm* enough for you, am I *giving*? Am I *pleasing* the woman I love?"

He gave her no chance to reply. He pushed her down on to the couch and she was sinking deeper and even more deeply into the boundlessness of his kiss, into the ocean depths of him. Through the sea haze came a whisper.

"My love, you *have* my love, I trust you as I trust no other woman. For God's sake—" They were lying together and his mouth was roaming her throat. "Tell me you love me and mean it this time!"

"I do, I do love you, Todd!" she gasped.

Fingers urged down the shoulder straps and somehow her arms were free. His lips moved lower, easing the dress away to free the full, enticing shape of her. In her ecstasy she cried out to him. Her hands gripped his head, her fingers moved over the dark hair. The metal of the necklace was imprinted on her skin by the pressure of his forehead.

His shoulder muscles rippled under her fingers and as she opened her mouth to gasp again at the audacity of his tongue upon the most sensitive part of her breasts, he moved to claim her lips, his hair-roughened chest abrasive against her body.

Their legs entangled and she knew of his male desire. She felt a craving to please, to give of herself whatever he wanted. Her body arched spontanteously against his and she was dimly aware of the fact that, in a few moments, it would be beyond her powers to alter the course events must take—that before many more minutes had passed, he would take her and make her his.

Softly she moaned and as his lips lifted, her mouth sought his almost desperately. He evaded her laughingly to tease, then his expression grew serious. "I'm not letting you escape me now," he said roughly. "Last time you pleaded with me to stay with you. This time I will. You'll belong to me. And afterward, I'll lie beside you and—"

He stopped, his head held stiffly as though listening.

"I heard something," he said, "from downstairs."

Alicia tensed uncomprehendingly. How could so much passion, she wondered sadly, die away so quickly?

"The neighbors, that's all," she sighed, hoping her suggestion would pacify him and bring him back to her.

"Not voices, and not a door closing."

"A thief in the night?" she asked lightly.

"Yes." The answer was uncompromising. His weight lifted from her, leaving her cold and exposed. The brown eyes that looked down on her were not those of a lover. Was there a hardness in them? If so, surely it wasn't meant for her? Not after those kisses and those precious moments they had shared.

It seemed he was not even seeing her. He was gone from her as surely as if he had already left the apartment.

There came a clatter of breaking glass—not of a broken window, but of wineglasses knocked flying by a careless movement in the darkness. Now Alicia was alert, swinging her legs to the floor, pulling her dress into place. Was Todd right after all? Had someone broken in?

Todd tucked in his shirt and grabbed the jacket of his suit, pulling it on as he ran down the stairs. Alicia's hands were shaking as they lifted, pressing into her flushed cheeks and smoothing her rumpled hair. What if Todd confronted an intruder and what if the man was dangerous? Feverishly seeking her evening sandals and pulling them on, she ran to the door. Halfway down, she paused. She had recognized one of the raised, arguing voices. Leonard Richardson was down there and, judging by the angry shouts, Todd had him by the throat.

CHAPTER TEN

THE SOUNDS CAME from the bedroom Todd used as an office. Within its four walls were secrets that Todd would be prepared to guard with his life. As Alicia stood irresolutely in Todd's living room, two figures emerged from the office.

Todd had Leonard's arm in a vicious backward hold. He forced his victim through the doorway and said, "Now, talk."

Leonard saw Alicia and his face, already contorted with the pain Todd was inflicting, twisted maliciously. "Ask her," he said through gritted teeth. "She knew I was coming."

"*I* knew?" Alicia gasped. "It's not true," she told Todd. "It's a miserable l—"

"I might, just might, call on you this evening," Leonard had said. An informal visit, she had visualized, friend to friend, a chat over coffee. . . .

Todd's jaw jutted in a kind of contemptuous fury. "So you did know."

"No, no! Well, yes, in a way, but—" Todd's breathing deepened threateningly. "Not in that way, Todd!" It was a strangled appeal for understanding.

"You little bitch." Each word came out slowly. "You had me up there, kept me there by every feminine weapon you possessed, waiting, waiting until Master Spy himself had done his job, not counting on my having acute hearing, no matter how far I might have got in my possession of your body—"

Leonard smiled, but it was a tight, strained thing. "Clever, aren't we?" he interposed. "Worked it out over our lunches together."

"He's lying, Todd!" Alicia said wildly.

"She's been working with me all along," Leonard persisted. "Giving me copies of secret reports, sometimes almost as soon as they were in her possession."

Todd's head swung to her. "Deny that if you can."

"I can! I do!" She was frightened now. Knowing full well of Todd's almost obsessional mistrust of womankind, remembering how, until recently, he had mistrusted her and cursed Halmar Seagar for letting her into his most precious secret of all, she knew that no amount of pleading her cause would make him believe in her innocence now.

"Right from the day he came whining to me about his low pay and status relative to his intellectual worth." Todd's look of scorn, directed at Leonard, caused the recipient to turn a dull red. Todd turned the contemptuous gaze onto Alicia. "He implicated you. Not by name. He was too aware of the laws of slander, having, it seemed, done his legal homework. A girl on the staff, he hinted, one he was friendly with. It took only a second or two to pinpoint who it was."

Alicia grasped at this straw. "I knew I was under suspicion, in your eyes, anyway. So I'd have been more careful, wouldn't I? I'd have got the information out of you by . . . by more subtle means." The toes of her partially-covered feet engrossed her. "You know how many . . . well, opportunities I had."

He released Leonard's arm so abruptly there was an ag-

onized shout. Todd walked, jaw thrust forward, to face
Alicia. "And I, *my little sweetheart*, was on my guard every
time we were in *intimate* contact. Suspicion doesn't blunt
a man's virility, sometimes it might even sharpen it."

He raked her shivering figure, and it was as if he were
tearing her crumpled dress from her, piece by piece, ripping
through everything until she stood uncovered and utterly
exposed. She grasped her elbows after pushing back a piece
of straying hair. The humiliation he had forced on her that
day in the office at the research laboratory hit her again,
and she felt like a leaf that had shriveled in a summer
drought.

"Didn't it occur to you, my love," Todd went on relentlessly, "that *I* might be using 'more subtle means'—my
arms and my lips—to elicit information from *you*?"

Alicia grew pale. "So everything you've said
about . . . about loving me was false? You didn't mean a
word—not even when you asked me to marry you?" His
arms folded across his chest in a now familiar gesture. He
waited. "Todd, I'm innocent of everything Leonard's accused me of, I swear."

Leonard said with twisted lips, "Look at the thing she's
wearing around her neck."

Alicia's hand went to her throat.

Todd's head turned slowly toward Leonard. "It belongs
to her mother, she said."

"Did she?" he sneered. "Well, she's lying. *I* bought it
for her. *I* gave it to her."

Todd's eyes were grim. "Prove it, you swine."

"I'll prove it. I'll prove it all right." Leonard's voice
rose a pitch. His hand was shaking as he searched the inside

pocket of his zip-fronted jacket. "Here. Look at this. This photograph." He pushed it into Todd's line of vision.

Alicia held her head. There was a pain in the pit of her stomach. The picture Leonard took of her putting on the necklace when they had tea at that café. He was using the photograph as evidence to support his insistence on her involvement. And she, fool that she was, had thought it had been as he said—a picture to remind himself of his successful efforts to better himself in life!

"You unprincipled cheat," she flung at Leonard, only to earn a triumphant smile from him.

"And what would you call yourself?" Todd asked with deceptive calmness. His hand indicated the necklace. "Your mother's, you told me."

"If I'd told you the truth," she returned defensively, "you . . . you'd have—"

His lips became a tight, red line. "I'd have killed you, you lying little hypocrite."

"*He* could be lying, couldn't he?" Her voice was almost a shriek.

"No, you don't, Alicia," Leonard cautioned. "I've got more proof. I'm careful, you see. I keep evidence to back up my stories."

"Stories, that's all they are!" No one heeded her outburst.

Todd was studying a piece of paper Leonard had thrust into his hands. "Proof indeed," commented Todd, eyes narrowing into burning slits. "The jeweler's receipt, cash paid. Exact description of goods sold. A three-figure sum— a lot to pay out on someone whose nose is clean, who's as innocent as a newborn babe, is it not?"

The receipt fluttered to the floor and Leonard scooped it up.

"You." Todd's hands fastened around Alicia's neck. "I'll deal with when I return. If you so much as put a foot outside this building before then, I'll make it so you won't get another job—*of any kind*—until the day you die."

His fingers tightened and her fear increased as the pain from the pressure grew worse. Tears sprang, her teeth savaged her lower lip. She knew of Todd's mercy—it was nonexistent when he chose, and he chose now. "If you ever let me down," he'd said. "If you so much as breathe a word about Sander Design to any other person, I'll do this until you cry out for mercy." And he had caught her by the throat as he had her now.

With frantic fingers she clawed at his hands. Leonard made no move to intervene on her behalf. It was his own skin he was intent on saving now.

Alicia was sure it was only Leonard's edging toward the door that saved her from being choked into total submission at Todd Alexander's hands. The pain of his loosened hold was, if anything, worse than the hold itself. Now she was choked with tears, tears that wouldn't come, that tore at her chest, that took the breath from her as she ran to the stairs and slumped when she reached the top.

"Come on, you bastard," she heard Todd say as he roughed Leonard out of the building and into his car.

Lying facedown on the bed, she sobbed into her pillow. "I trust you as I trust no other woman." Had he really spoken those words only a short while ago? Or had they simply been part of a beautiful dream?

DAWN WAS LIGHTENING the sky when footsteps on the stairs brought her out of her tortured dream. The bedroom light was still on. Her blue dress was even more rumpled.

Her head came up as she listened. Fear had her body so rigid she could not even shake. The living-room door was flung wide, the bedroom door likewise. Todd stood there, gazing at her. He looked disheveled, his tie was missing, his shirt open to the waist. His eyes seemed glazed, as if he had drunk too much alcohol.

Alicia knew a terror that petrified, that strangled even the scream in her throat. He looked murderous. Her legs swung down, her hands clutched her head as if to protect it, and she pulled it down to hide her face from any blow that might come her way.

"Do you really think I'd harm you?" The tone was not that of a drunken man, nor someone with physical blows in mind.

She would not be fooled. It was a ruse to get her to lower her guard, so she remained as she was. There were sounds of the bedroom chair creaking under someone's weight, but Alicia stayed on guard, tensed almost beyond endurance.

When at last she ventured to lift her head and look, she saw that Todd was sprawled, head back, eyes closed, arms hanging loosely, only a few feet away. The picture he presented was of utter exhaustion.

"You're exonerated," he muttered without changing his position. "Completely, totally cleared of all blame. Now will you stop cowering from me as if I were about to beat you up?" Warily she watched, not moving. "Because—" his head lifted a fraction and a pair of slitted eyes came to rest on her "—if you go on gazing at me as if brutality was my second name, I *will* beat you up. Get it?"

loosen. Her feet lifted to the bed and she lay back, her hair spread over the pillow, her arms upraised to rest on it, too.

"Did you beat Leonard up?" she queried tiredly. "Is that how you got him to talk?"

Todd roused himself from the chair and paced the room, hands in pockets. A piece of hair fell forward. Impatiently he raked it back.

"A bit of rough treatment was called for," Todd said. "Especially when he tried to twist and run. Then he aimed a couple of punches, which I easily dodged. I managed to get the office doorway blocked long enough to dial Halmar's number and my father's, not to mention getting two or three of my research friends out of their beds. They all made it in record time, traffic at that hour being thin on the roads."

After a pause, in which she thought he must surely wear a path on her carpet, she said, with a touch of fretfulness, "Mr. Seagar believed in me all the time."

"Meaning so should I?"

"Yes." She could afford to be blunt now. Yet the knowledge that her name had been cleared did not fill her with the euphoria she might have expected. It hadn't brought Todd any closer, nor had it produced from him those three longed-for words. Maybe she would never hear them.

"You have my love," he'd said earlier, but that was before Leonard had arrived, before those bitter accusations had been made. He'd call her then a "lying hypocrite," told her he'd used his arms and lips to trick her into confessing. But there had been nothing to confess, except her innocence in the matter, and he hadn't believed her when she had told him.

He came to the bed and gazed down at her. "I have to

say it," he said at last. "Even Halmar began to have his doubts."

Alicia's eyes grew troubled. "He did keep asking me about my friendship with Leonard."

"Maybe it was that thing—" he indicated the necklace "—that made him wonder."

"He must have guessed I was lying about its being my mother's."

Todd nodded.

She said fiercely, "I hated telling Mr. Seagar a lie. But something made me afraid of admitting Leonard gave it to me."

"Intuition, maybe?" Todd's smile was faintly teasing, but Alicia nodded seriously. Todd straightened. "There were so many pointers—the time I caught you whispering the words, 'Tell Leonard he's back,' on your telephone. And sure enough, a few minutes later, there was Richardson knocking on my door. The day you took him out of your office next to mine to talk secretly to him. . . . Yes, I took note of everything. The number of times you lunched with him. When I was away, I asked Halmar to watch you."

She sat up. "But the day I pulled Leonard outside was the time I was typing that cassette you gave me of that coversation you recorded with someone at the research lab. I was trying to *prevent* Leonard from hearing or seeing what the cassette had on it."

"That cassette—which incidentally was scientifically meaningless—was what the lab phoned me about in the early hours."

Alicia turned pink, remembering the circumstances. "That was when we—"

"Were getting on so well." He smiled and for a moment

the old mockery reappeared. "I cursed them for the interruption."

"I wondered why your attitude changed so much toward me after talking to them."

The angled outline of his shadowed jaw grew harder. "They told me that he—Leonard—had passed its contents on in record time. I assumed—" he looked down at her "—with your help."

"I'd finished transcribing it by lunchtime and locked it all in my desk. Somehow he must have got at it."

Todd sighed, resuming his restless walking. "That was only one of many incidents. There was the time, early on, when you took it on yourself to work in my room—before I gave you an office to yourself."

"I remember. I was typing the first secret report. Mr. Seagar had impressed on me that it was extremely confidential. I found your office empty and thought you wouldn't mind if I used it while you were out. When I shouted, 'No,' it was because I thought it was Leonard coming in. I'd had a suspicion he was snooping, and something—some instinct—warned me he wasn't to be trusted."

"Why didn't you tell me?" He was beside her again.

She studied the mountainlike slope her bended knees made under her rumpled blue dress. "I told you once . . . you scared me stiff!"

He laughed, and it was as if some of the tension was easing out of him. He lowered himself onto the bed.

"Carry on with the fairy story," she urged, glancing at him through her lashes.

"I'll carry on from where I left off, if you're not careful, before we were so rudely interrupted a few hours ago." The threat brought a smile to her pale face. Another glance showed her the increasing warmth in the brown eyes. The ice, she thought abstractedly, it's gone, it's been gone for a long time now. . . .

Then Todd frowned. "Every single report you typed was leaked," he continued, rising and pacing again.

Alicia sighed. "So the evidence mounted against me."

"And more that you don't know about. Richardson told the company to whom he passed the information that, since he was working with a partner—female—he wanted more money for his spying activities. He got it. Hence—" Todd nodded to the gold necklace "—the presentation of that to you."

"Guilty conscience on his part? If I'd known, I'd have thrown the thing back in his face."

She reached up and started to unfasten the clasp, but Todd's hand stopped her.

"Tell me something, Alicia." There was a cold sparkle in his gaze like moonlight on a coating of frost. "Why did you accept it from him?"

Why? She had dreaded the question. Would he believe what she told him now, any more than he had believed her earlier? A shiver seized her and her head lowered to rest on her knees. "When he gave it to me he said it was because I'd helped him. I said I hadn't really. He said he meant his career and I assumed it was the time I'd told him you were back and in that way, helped him get an interview with you."

"Why did you accept it?" The question came again, quietly, but the fear inside her was growing.

"When . . . when he took that picture," she answered falteringly, "he said it was so he could look at it and gloat about his success and his . . . his higher status in life. He said there was another reason why he bought it—as a way of saying, 'Thank you,' for my friendship. He hinted he'd have been really insulted if I'd refused to take it.''

"All of which put you under a moral obligation and forced you to accept?''

Had Todd understood at last? She looked hopefully up at him. "Yes, yes, that was what I was trying to say.'' Was there a softening in his eyes, even a look of relief?

He left the matter alone and went on, "All the time we worked on him, Leonard Richardson kept implicating you. Halmar didn't let up in his questioning, hoping to catch him out.'' Again he stopped beside her. "Your friend—my old and valued friend, Halmar—was prepared to carry on all night and all day, if necessary, to clear your name. His belief in your honesty was unswerving.''

Alicia smiled a little tearfully. "He's a wonderful man.''

"More 'wonderful' even than I am?'' The question was asked softly, mockingly.

"Yes.'' Her lip quivered. "He believed in me. You didn't.''

"My darling.'' He sat cornerwise on the bed. "Do you know the hell I've been through these last few weeks, trying—against all appearances and odds—to persuade myself of your innocence? One of the reasons I proposed marriage was because I thought that, as my wife-to-be, you'd be loyal to me and act only in my interests. But when every bit of so-called secret information you were given was still leaked, via Richardson, and knowing the only outside source in possession of that information was you, what could I do but go on suspecting you?''

Alicia lifted her shoulders and dropped them despondently. "So all those precious secrets have been given to your rivals? Which means you don't have the lead anymore in the field of electric storage batteries? That's terrible, Todd.''

Her voice was thick with misery and a deep-down sense of guilt, despite the fact that she knew she was innocent of treachery.

"No. The secrets are safe."

She stared at him. "But—but how? Why?''

"The rival 'company' with whom Richardson thought he was dealing told him that if he could get hold of valuable information of any kind that might help them gain a lead over us, they would not only reward him financially, they'd offer him a really well-paid job in the company, too.''

"And Leonard proceeded to oblige?''

"Right. But what he didn't know was that the 'company' was a fictitious one. The whole setup came into being with the help of my father. He invented its name, became its chairman, chief executive, head of the research division, the lot!''

"And do you mean Leonard never suspected!'' A warmth was creeping over her, of relief so immense she wanted to laugh and cry together.

"Not once. He got all the money he demanded, even for the 'partner' he claimed to have. Keep that thing.'' He nodded toward the necklace that she still wore. "It cost him a lot, and you deserve something from his ill-gotten gains for all the misery he put you through.''

She fingered the engraved gold links. "You don't mind?''

"Not if it gives you pleasure. And anyway, it was my money that enabled him to buy it!'' She looked at the bare finger of her left hand. He saw the action but made no comment.

Alicia frowned. "If you knew it was Leonard all the time, why did you keep him on? Why didn't you fire him?"

"Because it was imperative that we discover who the link man—or woman—was. Don't forget he implicated you from the beginning."

Alicia nodded. "He told me. But what really happened was that he picked on certain words I used by accident— like the time I told him some reports I had to type were confidential. That same morning, he'd heard Mr. Seagar whispering to me about typing some reports and warning me they were confidential. Leonard remembered them and if you hadn't given him what he thought was a better job, I'm sure he intended to use the information as a weapon to get what he wanted from you. He called it having a hold over you."

"The devious swine!" It took Todd a few minutes to recover from his anger. At last he became calmer and put his hand on her head, tipping it back so that he was looking into her eyes. "More than anything, I wanted you cleared. It took a lot longer than I ever thought it would."

"Maybe because I was innocent?" Her smile was intended to provoke.

"Ouch!" he said softly.

She smoothed her hair where he had ruffled it. "How did you finally get Leonard to talk?"

"By threatening to call the police. At which the squirming little swine informed his audience that, in this country at the present time, industrial espionage is not a criminal matter. So I said, 'Maybe not, but breaking and entering private premises is,' and I reached out to the telephone. He talked.''

Todd ran a hand over his face in a gesture of utter weariness.

"Would you like a drink, Todd?" Alicia ventured, hating to see the way exhaustion bowed his shoulders and painted deep shadows under his eyes. He nodded, adding, "The strongest you can find."

"I'll see what my father's got in his stock of drinks," she called over her shoulder, then returned, holding up a bottle for his inspection. He held out his hand, but she whisked it away. "Not the whole bottle. I'm not having you pass out on me."

"That," came a faintly derisive rejoinder, "I have no intention of doing."

When she returned, holding the glass, she found that he had stretched himself out full-length on her bed. He raised himself on an elbow to swallow the drink. Watching the liquid disappear inside him, she took the glass, then said, plaintively, "Please will you move over? I'm tired, too."

Smoothing the dress down to her ankles, she lay beside him. He watched the modest gesture with a crooked smile, then slipped an arm behind her back, but he did not pull her close.

"Want me to go on?" She nodded and he continued. "Richardson admitted he'd learned a technique for unlocking desk drawers without a key. He had also discovered that some filing cabinet keys were interchangeable and found one to fit yours. Thus he had access to every report you typed for me."

"I didn't even suspect that anyone had been tampering with anything," she said wonderingly.

"That was a technique he must have learned, too, Always cover your tracks. Incidentally. . . ." Was there the faintest drawl, a testing note? "How did Richardson know about the office here in my apartment?"

Alicia's mind sped back to the day Leonard had visited her. Had she told him then? No, since she hadn't even known about it herself until next day. "He—he must have picked it up from that conversation you taped with someone at the research lab, when I was standing by you. He's no fool," she added quickly, still hoping to convince him. "He told me so himself."

Todd laughed loudly at that and pulled her closer, but only for a moment. "Which makes him the biggest fool out. He didn't even know that the 'secrets' he was passing on were all phony, written completely in nonsensical scientific terms."

"Which means he didn't get anything at all out of the whole business, not a single useful piece of information? Oh, Todd, I'm so glad!" On impulse she rolled toward him, only to find there was no reponse in him toward her. Sadly, she rolled away.

He reached into his trouser pocket. "Give me your hand. Left, you little idiot, not right."

Open eyed, she obeyed and he flipped open the small box and took out a ring. Its cluster of diamonds dazzled her tired eyes, giving them some of their brightness.

As he slipped it on her engagement finger, he said, "With this ring I thee wed."

"Do you?" she whispered. "Not really. Not until—" To her astonishment, he made as if to remove the ring. In self-defense she clenched her hand. "Yes, yes, Todd, I—"

He half rolled toward her, onto his side. "You belong

to me. Okay?'' His eyes were smoldering. There was no doubting his desire, but what about the love?

"Todd—'' She searched for something to fill the tense silence. "If I was your number one suspect, why did you take me around the research lab that day?''

"To test if you would give its secrets away to Richardson.'' His lazy eyes were roaming her face.

"I didn't.''

"No, you didn't.''

It was becoming difficult to concentrate with Todd's warm eyes upon her. "I didn't tell him where the lab was, either.''

"You didn't know where it was. Could you tell *me* how to get there, for instance?''

Alicia frowned, realizing that it would be completely beyond her to direct anyone there, even herself!

"I wasn't that much of a fool,'' Todd added with a smug smile. "Remember I still suspected you.''

"Which is why—'' she couldn't meet his eyes "—you searched me so thoroughly before you dictated to me, I suppose?''

He smiled. "Why else?'' His roaming eyes made her feel as naked as she had been during the incident they were discussing.

Fiercely, she said, "I hated it.''

"Did you?'' There was amusement and doubt in the question.

"Yes.'' Wasn't she lying? she asked herself in anguish. "I've . . . I've never been so humiliated in my life. It was . . . it was awful.'' At last her eyes lifted. The look she found in his had her heart hammering.

His hand bunched under her chin. "Shall I order you to strip again?"

"No, no!" her lips said, but her eyes were wider with urgent longing and—surely it wasn't hope?

Cursing her body as a traitor, feeling it throbbing as desire rose like a cresting wave, she lay beside him as he rested on his elbow. Her eyes were hypnotized by his and she knew then that she would do anything he told her.

"Okay," he said softly, "strip for me."

As if mesmerized, her hands began to slide the straps from her shoulders and then her arms were free. Rolling onto her side, she tried to reach the back zipper, then felt his hands push hers away. The zipper came slowly down. She rolled onto her back again and started to ease the dress over her hips. His eyes had not left her, moving from her flushed face to the soft shapeliness of her, dwelling on her midriff and flat stomach—until she stopped abruptly.

It came to her like a blow from an unseen assailant just what she was doing. "With this ring I thee wed," he had intoned as he had place the engagement ring on her finger. But there had been no wedding! His vows never to marry, his statement that he'd take from a woman whatever she cared to give as long as it was outside the marriage ceremony, his mistrust of the female sex in general . . . .

Feverishly she attempted to pull the dress back, covering all of herself that she had, under the hypnotism of his eyes, bared to his sight. It was as though he had been expecting the action. He pounced, gripping her wrist with his hand, shifting across until his body covered hers, which necessitated freeing her wrists for a few seconds.

Using her freed hands, she gripped his shoulders that were hard under her frantic fingers. "I won't," she gasped,

"I won't give in. Engagement isn't marriage. You don't love me." Her struggles were having the opposite effect— that of making him press down upon her even harder. "I told you once," she persisted, choking now in the face of defeat, "I won't have the loving without the love. I'll never let you add me to your 'choose, use and discard' list."

His mouth, silencing her savagely, forced her lips to allow him access. His hands skimmed and molded, feathering her waist and coming up on her thighs. They came up against the barrier of the dress and with impatience, he broke off the kiss and moved onto his side. The beat of her heart was like a drum and it was beyond her powers to stop him.

Moments later the dress hit the floor. His shirt followed it. His smile was teasing. "Do you concede victory?" Mutely she shook her head. "What more must I do to make you—" He stopped and a knowing light flecked his brown eyes with gold. "No holds barred, my sweet?" His lips were moving against hers.

Having held herself tense against his strengthening desire, it was as much as she could do to prevent herself from relaxing into him and giving whatever he wanted. "No loving without the love, Todd," she said hoarsely. "I meant it then. I mean it now."

"How many times have you told me you love me?"

"How many times have you told me back?" she threw at him.

He buried his face in her neck and a shiver of excitement whispered through her. His lips touched and lifted, moving down, down, finding the thrusting softness of her, teasing, arousing, settling at last on the pink-tipped hardness until she cried out with a rushing release of joy.

Her hands gripped his body, feeling the hard muscles moving, the ribs ridged beneath the lean frame, searching to find the hair-covered wall of chest.

His voice was muffled as he asked, "Did I forget to tell you the other reason I asked you to marry me?"

Catching her breath, she nodded.

"How," he went on, "can you tell the woman you treasure above all else that you want her like a starving man a meal? That you need her like the heart needs a constant and unending supply of blood? If the words 'I love you' suffice in your eyes, then, love of my life, I'll say them. But," almost roughly, "to me no words can express the depth of my feelings for you. I want you, Alicia, here and now, I want you. My darling," he spoke thickly, "I need you. Are you going to tell me to wait until our wedding day?"

No words came to answer him, no shake of the head, only her hands pressing him close, and a murmured, "Love me, my love. Never let me go."

With their mouths locked, drinking joy from each other, Todd brought her desire and love for him to the moment of no return. It was a long time later that they emerged from the golden cloud of shared happiness.

Alicia murmured, with an impudence born of their new intimacy and knowledge of each other, "You really must stop kissing me, Mr. Alexander." Then with a sense of belonging that had her tied to him by an invisible but infinitely durable thread, she curled into him.

There was laughter deep in his throat. "I can kiss you from now until the end of the world," he whispered against her ear. He searched for her hand and his ring, finding it. "We're man and his woman now. My wife-to-be, my wife.

Maybe—'' he held her away and gazed deep into her eyes ''—just maybe, we'll rest for a while. But I can't put a length to the time. You see—'' he flicked her cheek beside her mouth ''—there's no other woman in my life at the moment.'' He added more seriously, ''Nor will there ever be again.''

''That empty picture frame, Todd?'' Her fingers made circles on his chest.

''There's a woman in it,'' he told her laughingly. ''That picture of you that Leonard Richardson took. I confiscated it. But on our wedding day, which for me can't be soon enough, there'll be two people in that frame. My wife— and her husband.''

''You,'' she added laughing and going into his out- stretched arms.

INTRODUCING

Harlequin Presents Collection

An exciting new series
of early favorites from

Harlequin Presents

This is a golden opportunity
to discover these best-selling beautiful
love stories — available once again
for your reading enjoyment...

because Harlequin understands
how you feel about love.

Harlequin Presents Collection

Available wherever Harlequin books are sold.

GREAT LOVE STORIES NEVER GROW OLD...

Like fine old Wedgwood, great love stories are timeless. The pleasure they bring does not decrease through the years. That's why Harlequin is proud to offer...

HARLEQUIN CLASSIC LIBRARY

Delightful old favorites from our early publishing program!

Each volume, first published more than 15 years ago, is an enchanting story of people in love. Each is beautifully bound in an exquisite Wedgwood-look cover. And all have the Harlequin magic, unchanged through the years!

Two **HARLEQUIN CLASSIC LIBRARY** volumes every month! Available NOW wherever Harlequin books are sold.